THE WORKS OF ANATOLE FRANCE
IN AN ENGLISH TRANSLATION
EDITED BY FREDERIC CHAPMAN

CRAINQUEBILLE
PUTOIS, RIQUET
AND OTHER PROFITABLE TALES

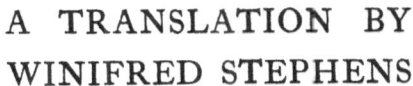

A TRANSLATION BY
WINIFRED STEPHENS

WILDSIDE PRESS

www.wildsidepress.com

TO

ALEXANDRE STEINLEN
AND TO
L U C I E N G U I T R Y
WHO, THE FORMER IN A SERIES OF
ADMIRABLE DRAWINGS, THE LATTER
IN A FINE DRAMATIC CREATION,
HAVE INVESTED WITH A TRAGIC
GREATNESS THE HUMBLE FIGURE
OF MY POOR COSTERMONGER

NOTE

The section entitled "Riquet" forms Chapter II of "Monsieur Bergeret à Paris" and is here included as an introduction to Riquet's "Meditations."

A story entitled "Onésime Dupont" appears both in the volume here presented and in the one entitled "Pierre Nozière." In the English edition it will be reproduced in the latter volume only.

CONTENTS

CRAINQUEBILLE

CRAINQUEBILLE

I

IN every sentence pronounced by a judge in the name of the sovereign people, dwells the whole majesty of justice. The august character of that justice was brought home to Jérôme Crainquebille, costermonger, when, accused of having insulted a policeman, he appeared in the police court. Having taken his place in the dock, he beheld in the imposing sombre hall magistrates, clerks, lawyers in their robes, the usher wearing his chains, *gendarmes,* and, behind a rail, the bare heads of the silent spectators. He, himself, occupied a raised seat, as if some sinister honour were conferred on the accused by his appearance before the magistrate. At the end of the hall, between two assessors, sat the Président Bourriche. The palm-leaves of an officer of the Academy decorated his breast. Over the

3

tribune were a bust representing the Republic and a crucifix, as if to indicate that all laws divine and human were suspended over Crainquebille's head. Such symbols naturally inspired him with terror. Not being gifted with a philosophic mind, he did not inquire the meaning of the bust and the crucifix; he did not ask how far Jesus and the symbolical bust harmonized in the Law Courts. Nevertheless, here was matter for reflection; for, after all, pontifical teaching and canon law are in many points opposed to the constitution of the Republic and to the civil code. So far as we know the Decretals have not been abolished. To-day, as formerly, the Church of Christ teaches that only those powers are lawful to which it has given its sanction. Now the French Republic claims to be independent of pontifical power. Crainquebille might reasonably say :

"Gentlemen and magistrates, in so much as President Loubet has not been anointed, the Christ, whose image is suspended over your heads, repudiates you through the voice of councils and of Popes. Either he is here to remind you of the rights of the Church, which invalidate yours, or His presence has no rational signification."

Whereupon President Bourriche might reply :

" Prisoner Crainquebille, the kings of France
have always quarrelled with the Pope. Guillaume
de Nogaret was excommunicated, but for so trifling
a reason he did not resign his office. The Christ of
the tribune is not the Christ of Gregory VII
or of Boniface VIII. He is, if you will, the Christ
of the Gospels, who knew not one word of canon
law, and had never heard of the holy Decretals."

Then Crainquebille might not without reason
have answered :

" The Christ of the Gospels was an agitator.
Moreover, he was the victim of a sentence, which
for nineteen hundred years all Christian peoples
have regarded as a grave judicial error. I defy you
Monsieur le Président, to condemn me in His name
to so much as forty-eight hours' imprisonment."

But Crainquebille did not indulge in any considerations either historical, political or social.
He was wrapped in amazement. All the ceremonial,
with which he was surrounded, impressed him with
a very lofty idea of justice. Filled with reverence,
overcome with terror, he was ready to submit to
his judges in the matter of his guilt. In his own
conscience he was convinced of his innocence ;
but he felt how insignificant is the conscience of a
costermonger in the face of the panoply of the law,

and the ministers of public prosecution. Already his lawyer had half persuaded him that he was not innocent.

A summary and hasty examination had brought out the charges under which he laboured.

II

CRAINQUEBILLE'S MISADVENTURE

P and down the town went Jérôme Crainquebille, costermonger, pushing his barrow before him and crying : " Cabbages ! Turnips ! Carrots ! " When he had leeks he cried : " Asparagus ! " For leeks are the asparagus of the poor. Now it happened that on October 20, at noon, as he was going down the Rue Montmartre, there came out of her shop the shoemaker's wife, Madame Bayard. She went up to Crainquebille's barrow and scornfully taking up a bundle of leeks, she said :

" I don't think much of your leeks. What do you want a bundle ? "

" Sevenpence halfpenny, mum, and the best in the market ! "

" Sevenpence halfpenny for three wretched leeks ? "

And disdainfully she cast the leeks back into the barrow.

Then it was that Constable 64 came and said to Crainquebille :

" Move on."

Moving on was what Crainquebille had been doing from morning till evening for fifty years. Such an order seemed right to him, and perfectly in accordance with the nature of things. Quite prepared to obey, he urged his customer to take what she wanted.

" You must give me time to choose," she retorted sharply.

Then she felt all the bundles of leeks over again. Finally, she selected the one she thought the best, and held it clasped to her bosom as saints in church pictures hold the palm of victory.

" I will give you sevenpence. That's quite enough ; and I'll have to fetch it from the shop, for I haven't anything on me."

Still embracing the leeks, she went back into the shop, whither she had been preceded by a customer, carrying a child.

Just at this moment Constable 64 said to Crainquebille for the second time :

" Move on."

" I'm waiting for my money," replied Crainquebille.

" And I'm not telling you to wait for your money ; I'm telling you to move on," retorted the constable grimly.

Meanwhile, the shoemaker's wife in her shop was fitting blue slippers on to a child of eighteen months, whose mother was in a hurry. And the green heads of the leeks were lying on the counter.

For the half century that he had been pushing his barrow through the streets, Crainquebille had been learning respect for authority. But now his position was a peculiar one : he was torn asunder between what was his due and what was his duty. His was not a judicial mind. He failed to understand that the possession of an individual's right in no way exonerated him from the performance of a social duty. He attached too great importance to his claim to receive sevenpence, and too little to the duty of pushing his barrow and moving on, for ever moving on. He stood still.

For the third time Constable 64 quietly and calmly ordered him to move on. Unlike Inspector Montauciel, whose habit it is to threaten constantly but never to take proceedings, Constable 64 is slow to threaten and quick to act. Such is his character. Though somewhat sly he is an excellent servant and a loyal soldier. He is as brave as a lion and as gentle

A

as a child.   He knows naught save his official instructions.

" Don't you understand when I tell you to move
on ? "

To Crainquebille's mind his reason for standing
still was too weighty for him not to consider it
sufficient.   Wherefore, artlessly and simply he
explained it :

" Good Lord !   Don't I tell you that I am waiting for my money."

Constable 64 merely replied :

" Do you want me to summons you ?   If you do
you have only to say so."

At these words Crainquebille slowly shrugged
his shoulders, looked sadly at the constable, and
then raised his eyes to heaven, as if he would say :

" I call God to witness !   Am I a law-breaker ?
Am I one to make light of the by-laws and ordinances which regulate my ambulatory calling ?
At five o'clock in the morning I was at the market.
Since seven, pushing my barrow and wearing my
hands to the bone, I have been crying : ' Cabbages !
Turnips !   Carrots ! '   I am turned sixty.   I am
worn out.   And you ask me whether I have raised
the black flag of rebellion.   You are mocking me
and your joking is cruel."

Either because he failed to notice the expression on Crainquebille's face, or because he considered it no excuse for disobedience, the constable inquired curtly and roughly whether he had been understood.

Now, just at that moment the block of traffic in the Rue Montmartre was at its worst. Carriages, drays, carts, omnibuses, trucks, jammed one against the other, seemed indissolubly welded together. From their quivering immobility proceeded shouts and oaths. Cabmen and butchers' boys grandiloquent and drawling insulted one another from a distance, and omnibus conductors, regarding Crainquebille as the cause of the block, called him " a dirty leek."

Meanwhile, on the pavement the curious were crowding round to listen to the dispute. Then the constable, finding himself the centre of attention, began to think it time to display his authority :

" Very well," he said, taking a stumpy pencil and a greasy notebook from his pocket.

Crainquebille persisted in his idea, obedient to a force within. Besides, it was now impossible for him either to move on or to draw back. The wheel of his barrow was unfortunately caught in that of a milkman's cart.

Tearing his hair beneath his cap he cried :

" But don't I tell you I'm waiting for my money ! Here's a fix ! *Misère de misère! Bon sang de bon sang !* "

By these words, expressive rather of despair than of rebellion, Constable 64 considered he had been insulted. And, because to his mind all insults must necessarily take the consecrated, regular, traditional, liturgical, ritual form so to speak of *Mort aux vaches*,* thus the offender's words were heard and understood by the constable.

" Ah ! You said : *Mort aux vaches.* Very good. Come along."

Stupefied with amazement and distress, Crainquebille opened his great rheumy eyes and gazed at Constable 64. With a broken voice proceeding now from the top of his head and now from the heels of his boots, he cried, with his arms folded over his blue blouse :

" I said ' *Mort aux vaches* ' ? I ? . . . Oh ! "

The tradesmen and errand boys hailed the arrest with laughter. It gratified the taste of all crowds for violent and ignoble spectacles. But

---

* It is impossible to translate this expression. As explained on p. 21, it means " down with spies," the word spies being used to indicate the police.

there was one serious person who was pushing his way through the throng ; he was a sad-looking old man, dressed in black, wearing a high hat ; he went up to the constable and said to him in a low voice very gently and firmly :

" You are mistaken. This man did not insult you."

" Mind your own business," replied the police-man, but without threatening, for he was speaking to a man who was well dressed.

The old man insisted calmly and tenaciously. And the policeman ordered him to make his declaration to the Police Commissioner.

Meanwhile Crainquebille was explaining :

" Then I did say ' *Mort aux vaches !* ' Oh !..."

As he was thus giving vent to his astonishment, Madame Bayard, the shoemaker's wife, came to him with sevenpence in her hand. But Constable 64 already had him by the collar ; so Madame Bayard, thinking that no debt could be due to a man who was being taken to the police-station, put her sevenpence into her apron pocket.

Then, suddenly beholding his barrow confiscated, his liberty lost, a gulf opening beneath him and the sky overcast, Crainquebille murmured :

" It can't be helped ! "

Before the Commissioner, the old gentleman declared that he had been hindered on his way by the block in the traffic, and so had witnessed the incident. He maintained that the policeman had not been insulted, and that he was labouring under a delusion. He gave his name and profession : Dr. David Matthieu, chief physician at the Ambroise-Paré Hospital, officer of the Legion of Honour. At another time such evidence would have been sufficient for the Commissioner. But just then men of science were regarded with suspicion in France.

Crainquebille continued under arrest. He passed the night in the lock-up. In the morning he was taken to the Police Court in the prison van.

He did not find prison either sad or humiliating. It seemed to him necessary. What struck him as he entered was the cleanliness of the walls and of the brick floor.

" Well, for a clean place, yes, it is a clean place. You might eat off the floor."

When he was left alone, he wanted to draw out his stool; but he perceived that it was fastened to the wall. He expressed his surprise aloud :

" That's a queer idea! Now there's a thing I should never have thought of, I'm sure."

Having sat down, he twiddled his thumbs and remained wrapped in amazement. The silence and the solitude overwhelmed him. The time seemed long. Anxiously he thought of his barrow, which had been confiscated with its load of cabbages, carrots, celery, dandelion and corn-salad. And he wondered, asking himself with alarm : " What have they done with my barrow ? "

On the third day he received a visit from his lawyer, Maître Lemerle, one of the youngest members of the Paris Bar, President of a section of La Ligue de la Patrie Française.

Crainquebille endeavoured to tell him his story ; but it was not easy, for he was not accustomed to conversation. With a little help he might perhaps have succeeded. But his lawyer shook his head doubtfully at everything he said ; and, turning over his papers, muttered :

" Hm ! Hm ! I don't find anything about all this in my brief."

Then, in a bored tone, twirling his fair moustache he said :

" In your own interest it would be advisable, perhaps, for you to confess. Your persistence in absolute denial seems to me extremely un-wise."

And from that moment Crainquebille would have made confession if he had known what to confess.

III

CRAINQUEBILLE BEFORE THE MAGISTRATES

RESIDENT BOURRICHE devoted six whole minutes to the examination of Crainquebille. This examination would have been more enlightening if the accused had replied to the questions asked him. But Crainquebille was unaccustomed to discussion; and in such a company his lips were sealed by reverence and fear. So he was silent : and the President answered his own question; his replies were staggering. He concluded : " Finally, you admit having said, '*Mort aux vaches.*' "

" I said, ' *Mort aux vaches !* ' because the policeman said, ' *Mort aux vaches !* ' so then I said ' *Mort aux vaches !* ' "

He meant that, being overwhelmed by the most unexpected of accusations, he had in his amazement merely repeated the curious words falsely attributed to him, and which he had certainly never pronounced. He had said, " *Mort aux vaches !* " as he might have said, " I capable of insulting anyone ! how could you believe it ? "

President Bourriche put a different interpretation on the incident.

" Do you maintain," he said, " that the policeman was, himself, the first to utter the exclamation ? "

Crainquebille gave up trying to explain. It was too difficult.

" You do not persist in your statement. You are quite right," said the President.

And he had the witness called.

Constable 64, by name Bastien Matra, swore he spoke the truth and nothing but the truth. Then he gave evidence in the following terms :

" I was on my beat on October 20, at noon, when I noticed in the Rue Montmartre a person who appeared to be a hawker, unduly blocking the traffic with his barrow opposite No. 328. Three times I intimated to him the order to move on, but he refused to comply. And when I gave him warning that I was about to charge him, he retorted by crying : ' *Mort aux vaches !* ' Which I took as an insult."

This evidence, delivered in a firm and moderate manner, the magistrates receied with obvious approbation. The witnesses for he defence were Madame Bayard, shoemaker's wife and Dr. David Matthieu, chief physician to the Hoital Ambroise Paré, officer of the Legion of Hcn r. Madame Bayard had seen nothing and heard n hing. Dr. Matthieu was in the crowd which had gathered round the policeman, who was ordering the coster-monger to move on. His evidence led to a new episode in the trial.

"I witnessed the incident," he said, "I observed that the constable had made a mistake; he had not been insulted. I went up to him and called his attention to the fact. The officer insisted on arresting the costermonger, and told me to follow him to the Commissioner of Police. This I did. Before the Commissioner, I repeated my declara-tion.

"You may sit down," said the President. "Usher, recall witness Matra."

"Matra, when you proceeded to arrest the accused, did not Dr. Matthieu point out to you that you were mistaken?"

"That is to say, Monsieur l Président, that he insulted me."

" What did he say ? "

" He said, ' *Mort aux vaches !* ' "

Uproarious laughter arose from the audience.

" You may withdraw," said the President hurriedly.

And he warned the public that if such unseemly demonstrations occurred again he would clear the court. Meanwhile, Counsel for the defence was haughtily fluttering the sleeves of his gown, and for the moment it was thought that Crainquebille would be acquitted.

Order having being restored, Maître Lemerle rose. He opened his pleading with a eulogy of policemen : " those unassuming servants of society who, in return for a trifling salary, endure fatigue and brave incessant danger with daily heroism. They were soldiers once, and soldiers they remain ; soldiers, that word expresses every-thing. . . ."

From this consideration Maître Lemerle went on to descant eloquently on the military virtues. He was one of those, he said, who would not allow a finger to be laid on the army, on that national army, to which he was so proud to belong.

The President bowed. Maître Lemerle happened to be lieutenant in the Reserves. He

was also nationalist candidate for Les Vieilles
Haudriettes.   He continued :

" No, indeed, I do not esteem lightly the in-
valuable services unassumingly rendered, which the
valiant people of Paris receive daily from the
guardians of the peace. And had I beheld in
Crainquebille, gentlemen, one who had insulted
an ex-soldier, I should never have consented to
represent him before you.   My client is accused
of having said : ' *Mort aux vaches !* ' The meaning of such an expression is clear. If you consult
Le Dictionnaire de la Langue Verte (slang) you will
find : ' *Vachard* a sluggard, an idler, one who
stretches himself out lazily like a cow instead of
working. *Vache*, one who sells himself to the
police ; spy.' *Mort aux vaches* is an expression
employed by certain people. But the question
resolves itself into this : how did Crainquebille
say it ? And, further, did he say it at all ?
Permit me to doubt it, gentlemen.

" I do not suspect Constable Matra of any evil
intention. But, as we have said, his calling is
arduous. He is sometimes harassed, fatigued,
overdone. In such conditions he may have suffered
from an aural hallucination. And, when he comes
and tells you, gentlemen, that Dr. David Matthieu,

officer of the Legion of Honour, chief physician at the Ambroise-Paré Hospital, a gentleman and a prince of science, cried : ' *Mort aux vaches*,' then we are forced to believe that Matra is obsessed, and if the term be not too strong, suffering from the mania of persecution.

" And even if Crainquebille did cry : ' *Mort aux vaches*,' it remains to be proved whether such words on his lips can be regarded as an offence. Crainquebille is the natural child of a costermonger, depraved by years of drinking and other evil courses. Crainquebille was born alcoholic. You behold him brutalized by sixty years of poverty. Gentlemen you must conclude that he is irresponsible."

Maître Lemerle sat down. Then President Bourriche muttered a sentence condemning Jérôme Crainquebille to pay fifty francs fine and to go to prison for a fortnight. The magistrates convicted him on the strength of the evidence given by Constable Matra.

As he was being taken down the long dark passage of the Palais, Crainquebille felt an intense desire for sympathy. He turned to the municipal guard who was his escort and called him three times :

" 'Cipal ! . . . 'cipal ! . . . Eh ! 'cipal ! " And he sighed :

" If anyone had told me only a fortnight ago that this would happen ! "

Then he reflected :

" They speak too quickly, these gentlemen. They speak well, but they speak too quickly. You can't make them understand you. . . . 'cipal, don't you think they speak too quickly ? "

But the soldier marched straight on without replying or turning his head.

Crainquebille asked him :

" Why don't you answer me ? "

The soldier was silent. And Crainquebille said bitterly :

" You would speak to a dog. Why not to me ? Do you never open your mouth ? Is it because your breath is foul ? "

IV

AN APOLOGY FOR PRESIDENT
BOURRICHE

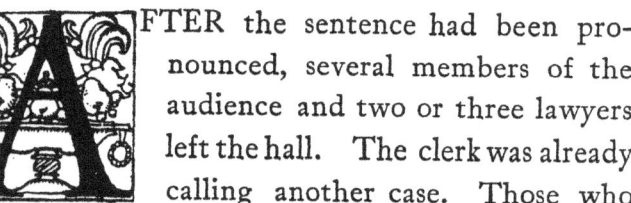FTER the sentence had been pro-
nounced, several members of the
audience and two or three lawyers
left the hall. The clerk was already
calling another case. Those who
went out did not reflect on the Crainquebille
affair, which had not greatly interested them; and
they thought no more about it. Monsieur Jean
Lermite, an etcher, who happened to be at the
Palais, was the only one who meditated on what he
had just seen and heard. Putting his arm on the
shoulder of Maître Joseph Aubarrée, he said:

"President Bourriche must be congratulated
on having kept his mind free from idle curiosity,
and from the intellectual pride which is determined
to know everything. If he had weighed one against
the other the contradictory evidence of Constable

24

Matra and Dr. David Matthieu, the magistrate
would have adopted a course leading to nothing
but doubt and uncertainty. The method of
examining facts in a critical spirit would be fatal
to the administration of justice. If the judge were
so imprudent as to follow that method, his sentences
would depend on his personal sagacity, of which he
has generally no very great store, and on human
infirmity which is universal. Where can he find a
criterion ? It cannot be denied that the historical
method is absolutely incapable of providing him
with the certainty he needs. In this connexion
you may recall a story told of Sir Walter Raleigh.

"'One day, when Raleigh, a prisoner in the
Tower of London, was working, as was his wont, at
the second part of his "History of the World," there
was a scuffle under his window. He went and
looked at the brawlers ; and when he returned to
his work, he thought he had observed them very
carefully. But on the morrow, having related the
incident to one of his friends who had witnessed
the affair and had even taken part in it, he was
contradicted by his friend on every point. Reflecting, therefore, that if he were mistaken as to
events which passed beneath his very eyes, how much
greater must be the difficulty of ascertaining the

truth concerning events far distant, he threw the
manuscript of his history into the fire.'

" If the judges had the same scruples as Sir
Walter Raleigh, they would throw all their notes
into the fire.   But they have no right to do so.
They would thus be flouting justice ; they would be
committing a crime.   We may despair of knowing,
we must not despair of judging.   Those who demand that sentences pronounced in Law Courts
should be founded upon a methodical examination
of facts, are dangerous sophists, and perfidious
enemies of justice both civil and military.   President Bourriche has too judicial a mind to permit
his sentences to depend on reason and knowledge,
the conclusions of which are eternally open to
question.   He founds them on dogma and moulds
them by tradition, so that the authority of his
sentences is equal to that of the Church's com-
mandments.   His sentences are indeed canonical.
I mean that he derives them from a certain number
of sacred canons.   See, for example, how he classifies
evidence, not according to the uncertain and deceptive qualities of appearances and of human veracity,
but according to intrinsic, permanent and manifest
qualities.   He weighs them in the scale, using weapons
of war for weights.   Can anything be at once simpler

and wiser ?   Irrefutable for him is the evidence
of a guardian of the peace, once his humanity
be abstracted, and he conceived as a registered
number, and according to the categories of an
ideal police.   Not that Matra (Bastien), born at
Cinto-Monte in Corsica, appears to him incapable
of error.   He never thought that Bastien Matra
was gifted with any great faculty of observation,
nor that he applied any secret and vigorous
method to the examination of facts.   In truth it
is not Bastien Matra he is considering, but Constable
64. A man is fallible, he thinks.   Peter and Paul
may be mistaken.   Descartes and Gassendi, Leibnitz
and Newton, Bichat and Claude Bernard were
capable of error.   We may all err and at any moment.
The causes of error are innumerable.   The percep-
tions of our senses and the judgment of our minds are
sources of illusion and causes of uncertainty.   We
dare not rely on the evidence of a single man : *Testis
unus, testis nullus.*   But we may have faith in a
number.   Bastien Matra, of Cinto-Monte, is fallible.
But Constable 64, when abstraction has been made
of his humanity, cannot err.   He is an entity.   An
entity has nothing in common with a man, it is free
from all that confuses, corrupts and deceives men.
It is pure, unchangeable and unalloyed.   Wherefore

the magistrates did not hesitate to reject the evidence
of the mere man, Dr. David Matthieu, and to admit
that of Constable 64, who is the pure idea, an emanation from divinity come down to the judgment bar.

" By following such a line of argument, President
Bourriche attains to a kind of infallibility, the only
kind to which a magistrate may aspire.   When the
man who bears witness is armed with a sword, it is
the sword's evidence that must be listened to, not
the man's.   The man is contemptible and may be
wrong.   The sword is not contemptible and is always
right.   President Bourriche has seen deeply into the
spirit of laws.   Society rests on force ; force must
be respected as the august foundation of society.
Justice is the administration of force.   President
Bourriche knows that Constable 64 is an integral part
of the Government.   The Government is immanent
in each one of its officers.   To slight the authority
of Constable 64 is to weaken the State.   To eat the
leaves of an artichoke is to eat the artichoke, as
Bossuet puts it in his sublime language.   (*Politique
tirée de l'Ecriture sainte, passim.*)

" All the swords of the State are turned in the
same direction.   To oppose one to the other is to
overthrow the Republic.   For that reason, Crainquebille, the accused, is justly condemned to a

fortnight in prison and a fine of fifty francs, on the evidence of Constable 64. I seem to hear President Bourriche, himself, explaining the high and noble considerations which inspired his sentence. I seem to hear him saying :

" 'I judged this person according to the evidence of Constable 64, because Constable 64 is the emanation of public force. And if you wish to prove my wisdom, imagine the consequences had I adopted the opposite course. You will see at once that it would have been absurd. For if my judgments were in opposition to force, they would never be executed. Notice, gentlemen, that judges are only obeyed when force is on their side. A judge without policemen would be but an idle dreamer. I should be doing myself an injury if I admitted a policeman to be in the wrong. Moreover, the very spirit of laws is in opposition to my doing so. To disarm the strong and to arm the weak would be to subvert that social order which it is my duty to preserve. Justice is the sanction of established injustice. Was justice ever seen to oppose conquerors and usurpers ? When an unlawful power arises, justice has only to recognize it and it becomes lawful. Form is everything ; and between crime and innocence there is but the thickness of a piece of stamped paper. It was for you, Crainquebille, to be the strongest. If, after having cried : " *Mort aux vaches !* " you had declared yourself emperor, dictator, President of the Republic or even town councillor, I assure you you would not have been sentenced to pass a fortnight in prison, and to pay a fine of fifty francs. I should have acquitted you. You may be sure of that.'

" Such would have doubtless been the words of President Bourriche ; for he has a judicial mind, and he knows what a magistrate owes to society. With order and regularity he defends social principles. Justice is social. Only wrong-headed persons would make justice out to be human and reasonable. Justice is administered upon fixed rules, not in obedience to physical emotions and flashes of intelligence. Above all things do not ask justice to be just, it has no need to be just since it is justice, and I might even say that the idea of just justice can have only arisen in the brains of an anarchist. True, President Magnaud pronounces just sentences ; but if they are reversed, that is still justice.

" The true judge weighs his evidence with weights that are weapons. So it was in the Crainquebille affair, and in other more famous cases."

Thus said Monsieur Jean Lermite as he paced up and down the Salle des Pas Perdus.

Scratching the tip of his nose, Maître Joseph Aubarrée, who knows the Palais well, replied :

" If you want to hear what I think, I don't believe that President Bourriche rose to so lofty a metaphysical plane. In my opinion, when he received as true the evidence of Constable 64, he merely acted according to precedent. Imitation lies at the root of most human actions. A respectable person is one who conforms to custom. People are called good when they do as others do."

V

CRAINQUEBILLE SUBMITS TO THE LAWS OF THE REPUBLIC

AVING been taken back to his prison, Crainquebille sat down on his chained stool, filled with astonishment and admiration. He, himself, was not quite sure whether the magistrates were mistaken. The tribunal had concealed its essential weakness beneath the majesty of form. He could not believe that he was in the right, as against magistrates whose reasons he had not understood: it was impossible for him to conceive that anything could go wrong in so elaborate a ceremony. For, unaccustomed to attending Mass or frequenting the Elysée, he had never in his life witnessed anything so grand as a police court trial. He was perfectly aware that he had never cried " *Mort aux vaches !* " That for having said it he should have been sentenced to a

fortnight's imprisonment seemed to him an august mystery, one of those articles of faith to which believers adhere without understanding them, an obscure, striking, adorable and terrible revelation.

This poor old man believed himself guilty of having mystically offended Constable 64, just as the little boy learning his first Catechism believes himself guilty of Eve's sin. His sentence had taught him that he had cried: "*Mort aux vaches!*" He must, therefore have cried "*Mort aux vaches!*" in some mysterious manner, unknown to himself. He was transported into a supernatural world. His trial was his apocalypse.

If he had no very clear idea of the offence, his idea of the penalty was still less clear. His sentence appeared to him a solemn and superior ritual, something dazzling and incomprehensible, which is not to be discussed, and for which one is neither to be praised nor pitied. If at that moment he had seen President Bourriche, with white wings and a halo round his forehead, coming down through a hole in the ceiling, he would not have been surprised at this new manifestation of judicial glory. He would have said: "This is my trial continuing!"

On the next day his lawyer visited him:

"Well, my good fellow, things aren't so bad after

c

all! Don't be discouraged. A fortnight is soon over. We have not much to complain of."

" As for that, I must say the gentlemen were very kind, very polite: not a single rude word. I shouldn't have believed it. And the *cipal* was wearing white gloves. Did you notice ? "

" Everything considered, we did well to confess."

" Perhaps."

" Crainquebille, I have a piece of good news for you. A charitable person, whose interest I have elicited on your behalf, gave me fifty francs for you. The sum will be used to pay your fine."

" When will you give me the money ? "

" It will be paid into the clerk's office. You need not trouble about it."

" It does not, matter. All the same I am very grateful to this person." And Crainquebille murmured meditatively: " It's something out of the common that's happening to me."

" Don't exaggerate, Crainquebille. Your case is by no means rare, far from it."

" You couldn't tell me where they've put my barrow ? "

VI

CRAINQUEBILLE IN THE LIGHT OF
PUBLIC OPINION

AFTER his discharge from prison, Crainquebille trundled his barrow along the Rue Montmartre, crying: " Cabbages, turnips, carrots ! " He was neither ashamed nor proud of his adventure. The memory of it was not painful. He classed it in his mind with dreams, travels and plays. But, above all things, he was glad to be walking in the mud, along the paved streets, and to see overhead the rainy sky as dirty as the gutter, the dear sky of the town. At every corner he stopped to have a drink ; then, gay and unconstrained, spitting in his hands in order to moisten his horny palms, he would seize the shafts and push on his barrow. Meanwhile a flight of sparrows, as poor and as early as he, seeking their livelihood in the road, flew off at the sound of his familiar cry:

" Cabbages, turnips, carrots ! " An old house wife, who had come up, said to him as she felt his celery :

" What's happened to you, Père Crainquebille ? We haven't seen you for three weeks. Have you been ill ? You look rather pale."

" I'll tell you, M'ame Mailloche, I've been doing the gentleman."

Nothing in his life changed, except that he went oftener to the pub, because he had an idea it was a holiday and that he had made the acquaintance of charitable folk. He returned to his garret rather gay. Stretched on his mattress he drew over him the sacks borrowed from the chestnut-seller at the corner which served him as blankets and he pondered : ' Well, prison is not so bad ; one has everything one wants there. But all the same one is better at home."

His contentment did not last long. He soon perceived that his customers looked at him askance.

" Fine celery, M'ame Cointreau !

" I don't want anything."

" What ! nothing ! do you live on air then ? "

And M'ame Cointreau without deigning to reply returned to the large bakery of which she was the mistress. The shopkeepers and caretakers, who had once flocked round his barrow all green and blooming, now turned away from him. Having reached the shoemaker's, at the sign of l'Ange Gardien, the place where his adventures with justice had begun, he called :

" M'ame Bayard, M'ame Bayard, you owe me sevenpence halfpenny from last time."

But M'ame Bayard, who was sitting at her counter, did not deign to turn her head.

The whole of the Rue Montmartre was aware that Père Crainquebille had been in prison, and the whole of the Rue Montmartre gave up his acquaintance. The rumour of his conviction had reached the Faubourg and the noisy corner of the Rue Richer. There, about noon, he perceived Madame Laure, a kind and faithful customer, leaning over the barrow of another costermonger, young Martin. She was feeling a large cabbage. Her hair shone in the sunlight like masses of golden threads loosely twisted. And young Martin, a nobody, a good-for-nothing, was protesting with his hand on his heart that there were no finer vegetables than his. At this sight Crainquebille's heart was rent. He pushed his barrow up to young Martin's, and in a plaintive broken voice said to Madame Laure: " It's not fair of you to forsake me."

As Madame Laure herself admitted, she was no

duchess.   It was not in society that she had acquired
her ideas of the prison van and the police-station.
But can one not be honest in every station in life ?
Every one has his self respect ; and one does not like
to deal with a man who has just come out of prison.
So the only notice she took of Crainquebille was to
give him a look of disgust.   And the old costermonger resenting the affront shouted :

"Dirty wench, go along with you."

Madame Laure let fall her cabbage and cried :

"Eh !   Be off with you, you bad penny.   You
come out of prison and then insult folk ! "

If Crainquebille had had any self-control he would
never have reproached Madame Laure with her
calling.   He knew only too well that one is not
master of one's fate, that one cannot always choose
one's occupation, and that good people may be
found everywhere.   He was accustomed discreetly
to ignore her customers' business with her ; and he
despised no one.   But he was beside himself.   Three
times he called Madame Laure drunkard, wench,
harridan.   A group of idlers gathered round Madame
Laure and Crainquebille.   They exchanged a few
more insults as serious as the first ; and they would
soon have exhausted their vocabulary, if a policeman
had not suddenly appeared, and at once, by his

silence and immobility, rendered them as silent and as motionless as himself. They separated. But this scene put the finishing touch to the discrediting of Crainquebille in the eyes of the Faubourg Mont-martre and the Rue Richer.

VII

RESULTS

THE old man went along mumbling:
" For certain she's a hussy, and
none more of a hussy than she."

But at the bottom of his heart
that was not the reproach he
brought against her. He did not scorn her
for being what she was. Rather he esteemed her
for it, knowing her to be frugal and orderly.
Once they had liked to talk together. She
used to tell him of her parents who lived in the
country. And they had both resolved to have a
little garden and keep poultry. She was a good
customer. And then to see her buying cabbages
from young Martin, a dirty, good-for-nothing
wretch; it cut him to the heart; and when she
pretended to despise him, that put his back up, and
then . . . !

But she, alas! was not the only one who shunned

him as if he had the plague.   Every one avoided him.
Just like Madame Laure, Madame Cointreau the
baker, Madame Bayard of l'Ange Gardien scorned
and repulsed him.   Why! the whole of society
refused to have anything to do with him.

So because one had been put away for a fortnight
one was not good enough even to sell leeks! Was
it just ?   Was it reasonable to make a decent chap
die of starvation because he had got into difficulties
with a copper ?   If he was not to be allowed to sell
vegetables then it was all over with him.   Like a
badly doctored wine he turned sour.   After having
had words with Madame Laure, he now had them
with every one.   For a mere nothing he would tell
his customers what he thought of them and in no
ambiguous terms, I assure you.   If they felt his
wares too long he would call them to their faces
chatterer, soft head.   Likewise at the wine-shop he
bawled at his comrades.   His friend, the chestnut-
seller, no longer recognized him ; old Père Crainquebille, he said, had turned into a regular porcupine.
It cannot be denied : he was becoming rude, dis-
agreeable, evil-mouthed, loquacious.   The truth of
the matter was that he was discovering the imper-
fections of society ; but he had not the facilities of
a Professor of Moral and Political Science for the

expression of his ideas concerning the vices of the system and the reforms necessary ; and his thoughts evolved devoid of order and moderation.

Misfortune was rendering him unjust. He was taking his revenge on those who did not wish him ill and sometimes on those who were weaker than he. One day he boxed Alphonse, the wine-seller's little boy, on the ear, because he had asked him what it was like to be sent away. Crainquebille struck him and said :

" Dirty brat ! it's your father who ought to be sent away instead of growing rich by selling poison."

A deed and a speech which did him no honour ; for, as the chestnut-seller justly remarked, one ought not to strike a child, neither should one reproach him with a father whom he has not chosen.

Crainquebille began to drink. The less money he earned the more brandy he drank. Formerly frugal and sober he himself marvelled at the change.

" I never used to be a waster," he said. " I suppose one doesn't improve as one grows old."

Sometimes he severely blamed himself for his misconduct and his laziness :

" Crainquebille, old chap, you ain't good for anything but liftin' your glass."

Sometimes he deceived himself and made out that he needed the drink.

"I must have it now and then; I must have a drop to strengthen me and cheer me up. It seems as if I had a fire in my inside; and there's nothing like the drink for quenching it."

It often happened that he missed the auction in the morning and so had to provide himself with damaged fruit and vegetables on credit. One day, feeling tired and discouraged, he left his barrow in its shed, and spent the livelong day hanging round the stall of Madame Rose, the tripe-seller, or lounging in and out of the wine-shops near the market. In the evening, sitting on a basket, he meditated and became conscious of his deterioration. He recalled the strength of his early years : the achievements of former days, the arduous labours and the glad evenings : those days quickly passing, all alike and fully occupied ; the pacing in the darkness up and down the Market pavement, waiting for the early auction ; the vegetables carried in armfuls and artistically arranged in the barrow ; the piping hot black coffee of Mère Théodore swallowed standing, and at one gulp ; the shafts grasped vigorously ; and then the loud cry, piercing as cock crow, rending the morning air as he passed through the crowded streets. All that innocent, rough life of the human pack-horse came before him. For half a century, on his travelling stall, he had borne to townsfolk worn with care and vigil the fresh harvest of kitchen gardens. Shaking his head he sighed :

" No ! I'm not what I was. I'm done for. The pitcher goes so often to the well that at last it comes home broken. And then I've never been the same since my affair with the magistrates. No, I'm not the man I was."

In short he was demoralized. And when a man reaches that condition he might as well be on the ground and unable to rise. All the passers-by tread him under foot.

VIII

THE FINAL RESULT

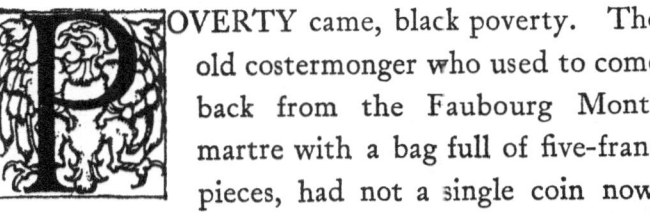OVERTY came, black poverty. The old costermonger who used to come back from the Faubourg Montmartre with a bag full of five-franc pieces, had not a single coin now. Winter came. Driven out of his garret, he slept under the carts in a shed. It had been raining for days ; the gutters were overflowing, and the shed was flooded.

Crouching in his barrow, over the pestilent water, in the company of spiders, rats and half-starved cats, he was meditating in the gloom. Having eaten nothing all day and no longer having the chestnut-seller's sacks for a covering, he recalled the fortnight when the Government had provided him with food and clothing. He envied the prisoners' fate. They suffer neither cold nor hunger, and an idea occurred to him :

" Since I know the trick why don't I use it ? "

He rose and went out into the street. It was a little past eleven. The night was dark and chill. A drizzling mist was falling, colder and more penetrating than rain. The few passers-by crept along under cover of the houses.

Crainquebille went past the Church of Saint-Eustache and turned into the Rue Montmartre. It was deserted. A guardian of the peace stood on the pavement, by the apse of the church. He was under a gas-lamp, and all around fell a fine rain looking reddish in the gaslight. It fell on to the policeman's hood. He looked chilled to the bone ; but, either because he preferred to be in the light or because he was tired of walking he stayed under the lamp, and perhaps it seemed to him a friend, a companion. In the loneliness of the night the flickering flame was his only entertainment. In his immobility he appeared hardly human. The reflection of his boots on the wet pavement, which looked like a lake, prolonged him downwards and gave him from a distance the air of some amphibious monster half out of water. Observed more closely he had at once a monkish and a military appearance. The coarse features of his countenance, magnified under the shadow of his hood, were sad and placid. He wore a thick moustache, short and grey. He was an old copper, a man of some two-score years. Crainquebille went up to him softly, and in a weak hesitating voice, said : " *Mort aux vaches !* "

Then he awaited the result of those sacred words. But nothing came of them. The constable remained motionless and silent, with his arms folded under his short cloak. His eyes were wide open ; they glistened in the darkness and regarded Crainquebille with sadness, vigilance and scorn.

Crainquebille, astonished, but still resolute, muttered :

" *Mort aux vaches !* I tell you."

There was a long silence in the chill darkness and the falling of the fine penetrating rain. At last the constable spoke :

" Such things are not said. . . . For sure and for certain they are not said. At your age you ought to know better. Pass on."

" Why don't you arrest me ? " asked Crainquebille.

The constable shook his head beneath his dripping hood :

" If we were to take up all the addle-pates who say what they oughtn't to, we should have our work cut out ! . . . And what would be the use of it ? "

Overcome by such magnanimous disdain, Crainquebille remained for some time stolid and silent, with his feet in the gutter. Before going, he tried to explain :

" I didn't mean to say : *Mort aux vaches !* to you. It was not for you more than for another. It was only an idea."

The constable replied sternly but kindly :

" Whether an idea or anything else it ought not to be said, because when a man does his duty and endures much, he ought not to be insulted with idle words. . . . I tell you again to pass on."

Crainquebille, with head bent and arms hanging limp, plunged into the rain and the darkness.

PUTOIS

TO GEORGES BRANDÈS

PUTOIS

I

HEN we were children, our tiny garden, which you could go from end to end of in twenty strides, seemed to us a vast universe, made up of joys and terrors," said Monsieur Bergeret.

"Do you remember Putois, Lucien ? " asked Zoé, smiling as was her wont, with lips compressed and her nose over her needlework.

"Do I remember Putois ! . . . Why, of all the figures which passed before my childhood's eyes, that of Putois remains the clearest in my memory. Not a single feature of his face or of his character have I forgotten. He had a long head. . . ."

"A low forehead," added Mademoiselle Zoé.

Then antiphonally, in a monotonous voice, with mock gravity, the brother and sister recited the following points of a kind of police description :

" A low forehead."

" Wall-eyed."

" Furtive looking."

" A crow's-foot on his temple."

" High cheek-bones, red and shiny."

" His ears were ragged."

" His face was blank and expressionless."

" It was only by his hands, which were constantly moving, that you divined his thoughts."

" Thin, rather bent, weak in appearance."

" In reality of unusual strength."

" He could easily bend a five-franc piece between his thumb and forefinger."

" His thumb was huge."

" He spoke with a drawl."

" His tone was unctuous."

Suddenly Monsieur Bergeret cried eagerly :

" Zoé ! We have forgotten his yellow hair and his scant beard. We must begin again."

Pauline had been listening with astonishment to this strange recital. She asked her father and her aunt how they had come to learn this prose passage by heart, and why they recited it like a Litany.

Monsieur Bergeret replied gravely :

" Pauline, what you have just heard is the sacred text, I may say the liturgy of the Bergeret family.

It is right that it should be transmitted to you in order that it may not perish with your aunt and me. Your grandfather, my child, your grandfather, Eloi Bergeret, who was not one to be amused with trifles, set a high value on this passage, principally on account of its origin. He entitled it 'The Anatomy of Putois.' And he was accustomed to say that in certain respects he set the anatomy of Putois above the anatomy of Quaresmeprenant. 'If the description written by Xenomanes,' he said, 'is more learned and richer in rare and precious terms, the description of Putois greatly excels it in the lucidity of its ideas and the clearness of its style.' Such was his opinion, for in those days Doctor Ledouble, of Tours, had not yet expounded chapters thirty, thirty-one and thirty-two of the fourth book of Rabelais."

" I can't understand you," said Pauline.

" It is because you don't know Putois, my daughter. You must learn that, in the childhood of your father and your aunt Zoé, there was no more familiar figure than Putois. In the home of your grand-father Bergeret, Putois was a household word. We all, in turn, believed that we had seen him."

" But who was Putois ? " asked Pauline.

Instead of replying her father began to laugh,

and Mademoiselle Bergeret also laughed, though her lips were closed.

Pauline looked first at one then at the other. It seemed to her odd that her aunt should laugh so heartily, and odder still that she should laugh at the same thing as her brother ; for strange to say the minds of the brother and sister moved in different grooves.

" Tell me who Putois was, papa. Since you want me to know, tell me."

" Putois, my child, was a gardener. The son of honest farmers of Artois, he had set up as a nursery-man at Saint-Omer. But he was unable to please his customers and failed in business. He gave up his nursery and went out to work by the day. His employers were not always satisfied."

At these words, Mademoiselle Bergeret, still laughing, remarked :

" You remember, Lucien, when father couldn't find his ink-pot, his pens, his sealing-wax or his scissors on his desk, how he used to say : ' I think Putois must have been here ?' "

" Ah ! " said Monsieur Bergeret, " Putois had not a good reputation."

" Is that all ? " asked Pauline.

" No, my child, it is not all. There was something

odd about Putois ; we knew him, he was familiar to
us and yet . . . . ”

. . . . “ He did not exist,” said Zoé.

Monsieur Bergeret looked reproachfully at her.

“ What a thing to say, Zoé !   Why thus break
the charm ?   Putois did not exist !   Dare you say so,
Zoé ?   Can you maintain it ?   Before affirming
that Putois did not exist, that Putois never was, you
should consider the conditions of being and the
modes of existence.   Putois existed, sister.   But it
is true that his was a peculiar existence.”

“ I understand less and less,” said Pauline, growing
discouraged.

“ The truth will dawn upon you directly, child.
Know that Putois was born in the fullness of age.
I was still a child ; your aunt was a little girl.   We
lived in a small house, in a suburb of Saint-Omer.
Our parents led a quiet retired life, until they were
discovered by an old lady of Saint-Omer, Madame
Cornouiller, who lived in her manor of Monplaisir,
some twelve miles from the town, and who turned
out to be my mother’s great aunt.   She took advantage of the privilege of friendship, to insist on our
father and mother coming to dine with her at
Monplaisir every Sunday.   There they were bored
to death.   But the old lady said it was right for

relatives to dine together on Sundays, and that only ill-bred persons neglected the observance of this ancient custom. Our father was miserable. His sufferings were pitiful to behold. But Madame Cornouiller did not see them. She saw nothing. My mother bore it better. She suffered as much as my father, and perhaps more, but she contrived to smile."

" Women are made to suffer," said Zoé.

" Every living creature in the world is born to suffer, Zoé. It was in vain that our parents refused these terrible invitations ; Madame Cornouiller's carriage came to fetch them every Sunday afternoon. They were bound to go to Monplaisir ; it was an obligation which they could not possibly avoid. It was an established order which only open rebellion could disturb. At length my father revolted, and swore he would not accept another of Madame Cornouiller's invitations. To my mother he left the task of finding decent pretexts and varying reasons for their repeated refusals ; it was a task for which she was ill fitted ; for she was incapable of dissimulation."

" Say rather, Lucien, that she was not willing to dissimulate. Had she wished she could have fibbed like anyone else."

"It is true that when she had good reasons she preferred giving them to inventing bad ones. You remember, sister, that one day she said at table : 'Fortunately Zoé has whooping-cough : so we shall not have to go to Monplaisir for a long time '."

"Yes, that did happen," said Zoé.

"You recovered, Zoé. And one day Madame Cornouiller came and said to our mother : 'My dear, I am counting on you and your husband coming to dine at Monplaisir on Sunday.' Our mother had been expressly enjoined by her husband to give Madame Cornouiller some plausible pretext for refusing. In her extremity the only excuse she could think of was absolutely devoid of probability : 'I am extremely sorry, madame, but it will be impossible. On Sunday I expect the gardener.'

"At these words Madame Cornouiller looked through the glazed door of the drawing-room at the wilderness of a little garden, where the spindle-trees and the lilacs looked as if they never had and never would make the acquaintance of a pruning-hook. 'You are expecting the gardener ! What for ? To work in your garden !'

"Then, our mother, having involuntarily cast eyes on the patch of rough grass and half-wild plants, which she had just called a garden, realized with alarm that her excuse must appear a mere invention. ' Why couldn't this man come on Monday or Tuesday to work in your . . . garden ?   Either of these days would be better.   It is wrong to work on Sunday.   Is he occupied during the week ? '

" I have often noticed that the most impudent and the most absurd reasons meet with the least resistance; they disconcert the opponent.   Madame Cornouiller insisted less than might have been expected of a person so disinclined to give in. Rising from her chair she asked : ' What is your gardener's name, dear ? '

" ' Putois,' replied our mother promptly.

" Putois had a name.   Henceforth he existed. Madame Cornouiller went off mumbling : ' Putois ! I seem to know that name.   Putois ? Putois ! Why, yes, I know him well enough.   But I can't recall him.   Where does he live ?   He goes out to work by the day.   When people want him, they send for him to some house where he is working.   Ah ! Just as I thought ; he is a loafer, a vagabond . . . a good-for-nothing.   You should beware of him, my dear.'

" Henceforth Putois had a character."

II

MONSIEUR GOUBIN and Monsieur Jean Marteau came in. Monsieur Bergeret told them the subject of the conversation :

"We were talking of the man whom my mother one day caused to exist, and created gardener at Saint-Omer. She gave him a name. Henceforth he acted."

"I beg you pardon, sir ?" said Monsieur Goubin, wiping his eye-glasses. "Do you mind saying that over again ?"

"Willingly," replied Monsieur Bergeret. "There was no gardener. The gardener did not exist. My mother said : 'I expect the gardener!' Straightway the gardener existed—and acted."

"But, Professor," inquired Monsieur Goubin, "how can he have acted if he did not exist ?"

"In a manner, he did exist," replied Monsieur Bergeret.

"You mean he existed in imagination," scornfully retorted Monsieur Goubin.

"And is not imaginary existence, existence?" exclaimed the Professor. "Are not mythical personages capable of influencing men? Think of mythology, Monsieur Goubin, and you will perceive that it is not the real characters, but rather the imaginary ones that exercise the profoundest and the most durable influence over our minds. In all times and in all lands, beings who were no more real than Putois, have inspired nations with love and hatred, with terror and hope, they have counselled crimes, they have received offerings, they have moulded manners and laws. Monsieur Goubin, think on the mythology of the ages. Putois is a mythological personage, obscure, I admit, and of the humblest order. The rude satyr, who used to sit at table with our northern peasants, was deemed worthy to figure in one of Jordaëns' pictures, and in a fable of La Fontaine. The hairy son of Sycorax was introduced into the sublime world of Shakespeare. Putois, less fortunate, will be for ever scorned by poets and artists. He is lacking in grandeur and mystery; he has no distinction, no character. He is the offspring of too rational a mind; he was conceived by persons who knew how to read and write, who lacked the enchanting imagination which gives birth to fables. Gentlemen, I think what I have said is enough to reveal to you the true nature of Putois."

"I understand it," said Monsieur Goubin.

Then Monsieur Bergeret continued :

"Putois existed. I maintain it. He was. Consider, gentlemen, and you will conclude that the condition of being in no way implies matter ; it signifies only the connexion between attribute and subject, it expresses merely a relation."

"Doubtless," said Jean Marteau, "but to be without attributes is to be practically nothing. Some one said long ago : 'I am that I am.' Pardon my bad memory ; but one can't recollect everything. Whoever it was who spoke thus committed a great imprudence. By those thoughtless words he implied that he was devoid of attributes and without relation, wherefore he asserted his own non-existence and rashly suppressed himself. I wager that he has never been heard of since."

"Then your wager is lost," replied Monsieur Bergeret. "He corrected the bad effect of those egotistical words by applying to himself a whole string of adjectives. He has been greatly talked of, but generally without much sense."

"I don't understand," said Monsieur Goubin.

"That does not matter," replied Jean Marteau.

And he requested Monsieur Bergeret to tell them about Putois.

" It is very kind of you to ask me," said the Professor. " Putois was born in the second half of the nineteenth century, at Saint-Omer. It would have been better for him had he been born some centuries earlier, in the Forest of Arden or in the Wood of Broceliande. He would then have been an evil spirit of extraordinary cleverness."

" A cup of tea, Monsieur Goubin," said Pauline.

" Was Putois an evil spirit then ? " inquired Jean Marteau.

" He was evil," replied Monsieur Bergeret ; " in a certain way, and yet not absolutely evil. He was like those devils who are said to be very wicked, but in whom, when one comes to know them, one discovers good qualities. I am disposed to think that justice has not been done to Putois. Madame Cornouiller was prejudiced against him ; she immediately suspected him of being a loafer, a drunkard, a thief. Then, reflecting that since he was employed by my mother, who was not rich, he could not ask for high pay, she wondered whether it might not be to her advantage to engage him in the place of her own gardener, who had a better reputation, but also, alas ! more requirements. It would soon be the

season for trimming the yew-trees. She thought
that if Madame Eloi Bergeret, who was poor, paid
Putois little, she who was rich might give him still
less, since it is the custom for the rich to pay less
than the poor. And already in her mind's eye she
beheld her yew-trees cut into walls, spheres and
pyramids, all for but a trifling outlay. ' I should look
after Putois,' she said to herself, ' and see that he did
not loaf and thieve. I risk nothing and save a good
deal. These casual labourers sometimes do better
than skilled workmen.' She resolved to make the
experiment, she said to my mother : ' Send Putois
to me, my dear. I will give him work at Monplaisir.'
My mother promised. She would willingly have
done it. But really it was impossible. Madame
Cornouiller expected Putois at Monplaisir and expected him in vain. She was a persistent person,
and, once having made a resolve, she was determined
to carry it out. When she saw my mother, she com-
plained of having heard nothing of Putois. ' Did
you not tell him, my dear, that I was expecting him?'
' Yes, but he is so strange, so erratic . . . ' Oh !
I know that sort of person. I know your Putois
through and through. But no workman can be so
mad as to refuse to come to work at Monplaisir.
My house is well known, I should think. Putois will

come for my instructions, and quickly, my dear. Only tell me where he lives ; and I will go and find him myself.' My mother replied that she did not know where Putois lived, he was not known to have a home, he was without an address. ' I have not seen him again, Madame. He seems to have gone into hiding.' She could not have come nearer the truth. And yet Madame Cornouiller listened to her with mistrust. She suspected her of beguiling Putois and keeping him out of sight for fear of losing him or rendering him more exacting. And she mentally pronounced her overselfish. Many a judgment generally accepted and ratified by history has no better foundation."

" That is quite true," said Pauline.

" What is true ? " asked Zoé, who was half asleep.

" That the judgments of history are often false. I remember, papa, that you said one day : ' It was very naïve of Madame Roland to appeal to an impartial posterity, and not to see that if her contemporaries were malevolent, those who came after them would be equally so.' "

" Pauline," inquired Mademoiselle Zoé, sternly, what has that to do with the story of Putois ? "

" A great deal, aunt."

" I don't see it."

Monsieur Bergeret, who did not object to digressions, replied to his daughter :

" If every injustice were ultimately repaired in this world, it would never have been necessary to invent another for the purpose. How can posterity judge the dead justly ? Into the shades whither they pass can they be pursued, can they there be questioned ? As soon as it is possible to regard them justly they are forgotten. But is it possible ever to be just ? What is justice ? At any rate, in the end, Madame Cornouiller was obliged to admit that my mother was not deceiving her, and that Putois was not to be found.

" Nevertheless, she did not give up looking for him. Of all her relations, friends, neighbours, servants and tradesmen she inquired whether they knew Putois. Only two or three replied that they had never heard of him. The majority thought they had seen him. ' I have heard the name,' said the cook, ' but I can't put a face to it.' ' Putois ! Why ! I know him very well,' said the road surveyor, scratching his ear. ' But I couldn't exactly point him out to you.' The most precise information came from Monsieur Blaise, the registrar, who declared that he had employed Putois to chop wood in his yard,

E

from the 19th until the 23rd of October, in the year
of the comet.

"One morning, Madame Cornouiller rushed
panting into my father's study : ' I have just seen
Putois,' she exclaimed. ' Ah ! Yes. I've just seen
him. Do I think so ? But I am sure. He was creep-
ing along by Monsieur Tenchant's wall. He turned
into the Rue des Abbesses ; he was walking quickly.
Then I lost him. Was it really he ? There's no
doubt of it. A man about fifty, thin, bent, looking
like a loafer, wearing a dirty blouse.' Such is indeed
Putois' description,' said my father. ' Ah ! I told
you so ! Besides, I called him. I cried : Putois !
and he turned round. That is what detectives do
when they want to make sure of the identity of a
criminal they are in search of. Didn't I tell you
it was he ! . . . I managed to get on his track, your
Putois. Well ! he is very evil looking. And it was
extremely imprudent of you and your wife to employ
him. I can read character ; and though I only saw
his back, I would swear that he is a thief, and perhaps
a murderer. His ears are ragged ; and that is an
infallible sign.' ' Ah ! you noticed that his ears were
ragged ? ' ' Nothing escapes me. My dear Monsieur
Bergeret, if you don't want to be murdered with
your wife and children, don't let Putois come into

your house again. Take my advice and have all your locks changed.'

" Now a few days later it happened that Madame Cornouiller had three melons stolen from her kitchen garden. As the thief was not discovered, she suspected Putois. The *gendarmes* were summoned to Monplaisir, and their statements confirmed Madame Cornouiller's suspicions. Just then gangs of thieves were prowling around the gardens of the country-side. But this time the theft seemed to have been committed by a single person, and with extraordinary skill. He had not damaged anything, and had left no footprint on the moist ground. The delinquent could be none other than Putois. Such was the opinion of the police sergeant; who had long known all about Putois, and was making every effort to put his hand on the fellow.

" In the *Journal de Saint-Omer* appeared an article on the three melons of Madame Cornouiller. It contained a description of Putois, according to information obtained in the town. ' His forehead is low,' said the newspaper, ' he is wall-eyed; his look is shifty, he has a crow's foot on the temple, high cheek-bones red and shiny. His ears are ragged. Thin, slightly bent, weak in appearance, in reality he is extraordinarily strong : he can easily bend a five-franc piece between his thumb and fore-finger.

" 'There were good reasons,' said the newspaper, 'for attributing to him a long series of robberies perpetrated with marvellous skill.'

" Putois was the talk of the town. One day it was said that he had been arrested and committed to prison. But it was soon discovered that the man who had been taken for Putois was a pedlar named Rigobert. As nothing could be proved against him, he was discharged after a fortnight's precautionary detention. And still Putois could not be found. Madame Cornouiller fell a victim to another robbery still more audacious than the first. Three silver teaspoons were stolen from her sideboard.

" She recognized the hand of Putois, had a chain put on her bedroom door and lay awake at night."

BOUT ten o'clock, when Pauline had gone to bed, Mademoiselle Bergeret said to her brother :

"Don't forget to tell how Putois seduced Madame Cornouiller's cook."

"I was just thinking of it, sister," replied her brother. "To omit that incident would be to omit the best part of the story. But we must come to it in its proper place. The police made a careful search for Putois but they did not find him. When it was known that he could not be found, every one made it a point of honour to discover him ; and the malicious succeeded. As there were not a few malicious folk at Saint-Omer and in the neighbourhood, Putois was observed at one and the same time in street, field and wood. Thus, another trait was added to his character. To him was attributed that gift of ubiquity which is possessed by so many popular heroes. A being capable of travelling long distances in a moment, and of appearing suddenly in the place where he is least expected, is naturally alarming. Putois was the terror of Saint-Omer. Madame Cornouiller, convinced that Putois had robbed her of three melons and three teaspoons, barricaded herself at Monplaisir and lived in perpetual fear. Bars, bolts and locks were powerless to reassure her. Putois was for her a terribly subtle creature, who could pass through closed doors. A domestic event redoubled her alarm. Her cook was seduced; and a time came when she could conceal her fault no longer. But she obstinately refused to indicate her betrayer.

" Her name was Gudule," said Mademoiselle Zoé.

" Her name was Gudule; and she was thought to be protected against the perils of love by a long and forked beard. A beard, which suddenly appeared on the chin of that saintly royal maiden venerated at Prague, protected her virginity. A beard, which was no longer young, sufficed not to protect the virtue of Gudule. Madame Cornouiller urged Gudule to utter the name of the man who had betrayed her and then abandoned her to distress. Gudule burst into tears, but refused to speak. Threats and entreaties were alike useless. Madame

Cornouiller made a long and minute inquiry. She diplomatically questioned her neighbours—both men and women—the tradesmen, the gardener, the road surveyor, the *gendarmes ;* nothing put her on the track of the culprit. Again she endeavoured to extract a full confession from Gudule. ' In your own interest, Gudule, tell me who it is.' Gudule remained silent. Suddenly Madame Cornouiller had a flash of enlightenment : ' It is Putois ! ' The cook wept and said nothing. ' It is Putois ! Why did I not guess it before ? It is Putois ! You unhappy girl ! Oh you poor, unhappy girl ! '

" Henceforth Madame Cornouiller was persuaded that Putois was the father of her cook's child. Every one at Saint-Omer, from the President of the Tribunal to the lamplighter's mongrel dog, knew Gudule and her basket. The news that Putois had seduced Gudule filled the town with laughter, astonishment and admiration. Putois was hailed as an irresistible lady-killer and the lover of the eleven thousand virgins. On these slight grounds there was ascribed to him the paternity of five or six other children born that year, who, considering the happiness that awaited them and the joy they brought to their mothers, would have done just as well not to put in an appearance. Among others were included the servant of Monsieur Maréchal, who kept the general shop with the sign of ' Le Rendezvous des Pêcheurs,' a baker's errand girl, and the little cripple of the Pont-Biquet, who had all fallen victims to Putois' charms. ' The monster !' cried the gossips.

" Thus Putois, invisible satyr, threatened with woes irretrievable all the maidens of a town, wherein, according to the oldest inhabitants, virgins had from time immemorial lived free from danger.

" Though celebrated thus throughout the city and its neighbourhood, he continued in a subtle manner to be associated especially with our home. He passed by our door, and it was believed that from time to time he climbed over our garden wall. He was never seen face to face. But we were constantly recognizing his shadow, his voice, his footprints. More than once, in the twilight, we thought we saw his back at the bend of the road. My sister and I were changing our opinions of him. He remained wicked and malevolent, but he was becoming child-like and simple. He was growing less real, and, if I may say so, more poetical. He was about to be included in the naïve cycle of children's fairy tales. He was turning into Croquemitaine, into Père Fouet-tard, into the dustman who shuts little children's eyes at night. He was not that sprite who by night

entangles the colt's tail in the stable. Not so rustic
or so charming, yet he was just as frankly mischievous;
he used to draw ink moustaches on my sister's dolls.
In our beds we used to hear him before we went to
sleep: he was caterwauling on the roofs with the cats,
he was barking with the dogs; he was groaning in
the mill-hopper; he was mimicking the songs of
belated drunkards in the street.

"What rendered Putois present and familiar to
us, what interested us in him was that his memory
was associated with all the objects that surrounded
us. Zoé's dolls, my exercise-books, the pages of
which he had so often blotted and crumpled, the
garden wall over which we had seen his red eyes
gleam in the shadow, the blue flower-pot one winter's
night cracked by him if it were not by the frost;
trees, streets, benches, everything reminded us of
Putois, our Putois, the children's Putois, a being
local and mythical. In grace and in poetry he fell
far short of the most awkward wild man of the woods,
of the uncouthest Sicilian or Thessalian faun. But
he was a demi-god all the same.

"To our father Putois' character appeared very
differently, it was symbolical and had a philosophical
signification. Our father had a vast pity for
humanity. He did not think men very reasonable.

Their errors, when they were not cruel, entertained and amused him. The belief in Putois interested him as a compendium and abridgment of all the beliefs of humanity. Our father was ironical and sarcastic; he spoke of Putois as if he were an actual being. He was sometimes so persistent, and described each detail with such precision, that our mother was quite astonished. 'Anyone would say that you are serious, my love, she would say frankly, and yet you know perfectly . . . .' He replied gravely 'The whole of Saint-Omer believes in the existence of Putois. Could I be a good citizen and deny it? One must think well before suppressing an article of universal belief.'

" Only very clear-headed persons are troubled by such scruples. At heart my father was a follower of Gassendi. He compromised between his individual views and those of the public: with the Saint-Omerites he believed in the existence of Putois, but he did not admit his direct intervention in the theft of the melons and the seduction of the cook. In short, like a good citizen he professed his faith in the existence of Putois, and he dispensed with Putois when explaining the events which happened in the town. Wherefore, in this case as in all others, he proved himself a good man and a thoughtful.

" As for our mother, she felt herself in a way responsible for the birth of Putois, and she was right. For in reality Putois was born of our mother's taradiddle, as Caliban was born of a poet's invention. The two crimes, of course, differed greatly in magnitude, and my mother's guilt was not so great as Shakespeare's. Nevertheless, she was alarmed and dismayed at seeing so tiny a falsehood grow indefinitely, and so trifling a deception meet with a success so prodigious that it stopped nowhere, spread throughout the whole town, and threatened to spread throughout the whole world. One day she grew pale, believing that she was about to see her fib rise in person before her. On that day, her servant, who was new to the house and neighbourhood, came and told her that a man was asking for her. He wanted he said, to speak to Madame. ' What kind of a man is he ? ' ' A man in a blouse. He looked like a country labourer. ' ' Did he give his name ? ' ' Yes, Madame.' ' Well, what is it ? ' ' Putois.' ' Did he tell you that that was his name?' ' Putois, yes Madame.' ' And he is here ? ' ' Yes, Madame. He is waiting in the kitchen.' ' You have seen him ? ' ' Yes, Madame.' ' What does he want ? ' ' He did not say. He will only tell Madame.' ' Go and ask him.'

" When the servant returned to the kitchen, Putois was no longer there. This meeting between Putois and the new servant was never explained. But I think that from that day my mother began to believe that Putois might possibly exist, and that perhaps she had not invented."

RIQUET

TO A. J.-A. COULANGHEON

RIQUET

UARTER-DAY had come. With his sister and daughter, Monsieur Bergeret was leaving the dilapidated old house in the Rue de Seine to take up his abode in a modern flat in the Rue de Vaugirard. Such was the decision of Zoé and the Fates.

During the long hours of the morning, Riquet wandered sadly through the devastated rooms. His most cherished habits were upset. Strange men, badly dressed, rude and foul-mouthed, disturbed his repose. They penetrated even to the kitchen where they stepped into his dish of biscuit and his bowl of fresh water. The chairs were carried off as fast as he curled himself up on them; the carpets were pulled roughly from under his weary limbs. There was no abiding-place for him, not even in his own home.

To his credit, be it said, that at first he attempted resistance. When the cistern was carried off he

barked furiously at the enemy. But no one re-
sponded to his appeal; no one encouraged him,
there was no doubt about it his efforts were regarded
with disapproval. Mademoiselle Zoé said to him
sharply : " Be quiet ! " And Mademoiselle Pauline
added : " Riquet, you are silly ! "

Henceforth he would abstain from useless warn-
ings. He would cease to strive alone for the public
weal. In silence he deplored the devastation of the
household. From room to room he sought in vain
for a little quiet. When the furniture removers
penetrated into a room where he had taken refuge, he
prudently hid beneath an as yet unmolested table or
chest of drawers. But this precaution proved worse
than useless ; for soon the piece of furniture tottered
over him, rose, then fell with a crash threatening to
crush him. Terrified, with his hair all turned up
the wrong way, he fled to another refuge no safer
than the first.

But these inconveniences and even dangers were
as nothing to the agony he was suffering at heart.
His sentiments were the most deeply affected.

The household furniture he regarded not as things
inert, but as living benevolent creatures, beneficent
spirits, whose departure foreshadowed cruel misfortunes. Dishes, sugar-basins, pots and pans, all

the kitchen divinities ; arm-chairs, carpets, cushions,
all the fetishes of the hearth, its lares and its domestic
gods had vanished.   He could not believe that so
great a disaster would ever be repaired.   And sorrow
filled his little heart to overflowing.   Fortunately
Riquet's heart resembled human hearts in being
easily distracted and quick to forget its misfortunes.

During the long absence of the thirsty workmen,
when old Angélique's broom raised ancient dust
from the floor, Riquet breathed an odour of
mice and watched the flight of a spider ; thus was
his versatile mind diverted.   But he soon relapsed
into sadness.

On the day of departure, when he beheld things
growing hourly worse and worse, he grew desperate.
It seemed to him above all things disastrous when
he saw the linen being piled in dark cases.   Pauline
with eager haste was putting her frocks into a trunk.
He turned away from her, as if she were doing something wrong.   He shrank up against the wall and
thought to himself : " Now the worst has come ;
this is the end of everything."   Then, whether it
were that he believed things ceased to exist when he
did not see them, or whether he was simply avoiding
a painful sight, he took care not to look in Pauline's
direction.   It chanced that as she was passing to and

fro she noticed Riquet's attitude. It was sad : but
to her it seemed funny, and she began to laugh.
Then, still laughing, she called out : " Come here !
Riquet, come to me ! " But he did not stir from his
corner, and would not even turn his head. He was
not then in the mood to caress his young mistress,
and, through some secret instinct, through a kind
of presentiment, he was afraid of approaching the
gaping trunk. Pauline called him several times.
Then, as he did not respond, she went and took him
up in her arms. " How unhappy we are ! " she
said to him ; " what is wrong then ? " Her tone
was ironical. Riquet did not understand irony.
He lay in Pauline's arms, sad and inert, affecting to
see nothing and to hear nothing. " Riquet, look
at me ! " She said it three times and three times
in vain. Then, pretending to be in a rage : " Silly
creature," she cried, " in with you " ; and she threw
him into the trunk and shut the lid on him. At that
moment her aunt having called her, she went out
of the room, leaving Riquet in the trunk.

He was seized with wild alarm ; for he was very
far from supposing that he had been playfully thrown
into the trunk for a mere joke. Esteeming his situation about as bad as it could be, he was desirous not
to make it worse by any imprudence. So he re-

mained motionless for a few moments, holding his breath. Then he deemed it expedient to explore his dark prison. With his paws he felt the skirts and the linen on to which he had been so cruelly precipitated, endeavouring to find some way out of this terrible place. He had been thus engaged for two or three minutes, when he was called by Monsieur Bergeret, who had been getting ready to go out.

"Riquet! Riquet! Come for a walk on the quays, that is the land of glory. True they have disfigured it by erecting a railway station of hideous proportions and striking ugliness. Architecture is a lost art. They have pulled down a nice looking house at the corner of the Rue du Bac. They will doubtless put some unsightly building in its place. I trust that at least our architects may abstain from introducing on to the Quai d'Orsay that barbarous style of which they have given such a horrid example at the corner of the Rue Washington and the Champs Élysées! . . . . Riquet! Riquet! Come for a walk on the quays. That is a glorious land. But architecture has deteriorated sadly since the days of Gabriel and of Louis. . . . . Where is the dog? . . . Riquet! Riquet!"

The sound of Monsieur Bergeret's voice was a great consolation to Riquet. He replied by making a noise with his paws, scratching frantically against the wicker sides of the trunk.

"Where is the dog?" her father asked Pauline as she was returning with a pile of linen in her arms.

"He is in the trunk, Papa."

"What, in the trunk! Why is he there?" asked Monsieur Bergeret.

"Because he was silly," replied Pauline.

Monsieur Bergeret liberated his friend. Riquet followed him into the hall, wagging his tail. Then a sudden thought occurred to him. He went back into the room, ran up to Pauline and rubbed against her skirt. And not until he had wildly caressed her as evidence of his loyalty did he rejoin his master on the staircase. He would have felt himself deficient in wisdom and religious feeling had he failed to display these signs of affection to one who had been so powerful as to plunge him into a deep trunk.

In the street, Monsieur Bergeret and his dog beheld the sad sight of their household furniture scattered over the pavement. The removers had gone off to the public-house round the corner, leaving the plate-glass mirror of Mademoiselle Zoé's wardrobe to reflect the passing procession of girls, workmen, shop-keepers, and Beaux Arts students, of drays, carts and cabs, and the chemist's shop with its bottles and its serpents of Æsculapius.   Leaning against a post was Monsieur Bergeret senior, smiling in his frame, mild, pale and delicate looking, with his hair ruffled. With affectionate respect the son contemplated his parent whom he moved away from the post.   He likewise lifted out of harm's way Zoé's little table, which looked ashamed at finding itself in the street.

Meanwhile Riquet was patting his master's legs with his paws, looking up at him with sorrowing beautiful eyes, which seemed to say :

" Thou, who wert once so rich and so powerful, canst thou have become poor ?   Canst thou have lost thy power, O my Master ?   Thou permittest men clothed in vile rags to invade thy sitting-room, thy bedroom, thy dining-room, to throw themselves upon thy furniture and pull it out of doors, to drag down the staircase thy deep arm-chair, thy chair and mine, for in it we repose side by side in the evening and sometimes in the morning too.   I heard it groan in the arms of those tatterdemalions ; that chair which is a fetish and a benignant spirit.   Thou didst offer no resistance to the invaders.   But if thou dost no longer possess any of those genii who once filled thy dwelling, if thou hast lost all, even those little divinities, which thou didst put on in the morning when getting out of bed, those slippers which I used to bite in my play, if thou art indigent and poor, O my Master, then what will become of me ? "

THE MEDITATIONS OF RIQUET

THE MEDITATIONS OF RIQUET

I

EN, beasts and stones grow great as they come near and loom enormous when they are upon me. It is not so with me. I remain equally great wheresoever I am.

II

When my master places for me beneath the table the food which he was about to put into his own mouth, it is in order that he may tempt me and that he may punish me if I yield to temptation. For I cannot believe that he would deny himself for my sake.

III

The smell of dogs is sweet in the nostrils.

IV

My master keeps me warm when I lie behind him in his chair.   It is because he is a god.   In front of the fire-place is a hot stone.   That stone is divine.

V

I speak when I please.   From my master's mouth proceed likewise sounds which make sense.   But his meaning is not so clear as that expressed by the sounds of my voice.   Every sound that I utter has a meaning.   From my master's lips come forth many idle noises.   It is difficult but necessary to divine the thoughts of the master.

VI

To eat is good.   To have eaten is better.   For the enemy who lieth in wait to take your food is quick and crafty.

VII

All is flux and reflux.   I alone remain.

VIII

I am in the centre of all things ; men, beasts and things, friendly and adverse, are ranged about me.

IX

In sleep one beholdeth men, dogs, horses, trees, forms pleasant and unpleasant.   When one awaketh these forms have vanished.

X

Reflection.   I love my master, Bergeret, because he is powerful and terrible.

XI

An action for which one has been beaten is a bad action.   An action for which one has received caresses or food is a good action.

XII

At nightfall evil powers prowl round the house. I bark in order that my master may be warned and drive them away.

XIII

Prayer. O my master, Bergeret, god of courage, I adore thee. When thou art terrible, be thou praised. When thou art kind be thou praised. I crouch at thy feet : I lick thy hands. When, seated before thy table spread, thou devourest meats in abundance, thou art very great and very beautiful. Very great art thou and very beautiful when, striking fire out of a thin splint of wood, thou changest night into day. Keep me in thine house and keep out every other dog. And thou, Angélique, the cook, divinity good and great, I fear thee and I venerate thee in order that thou mayest give me much to eat.

XIV

A dog who lacketh piety towards men and who scorneth the fetishes assembled in his master's house liveth a miserable and a wandering life.

XV

One day, from a broken pitcher, filled with water which was being carried across the parlour, water

ran on to the polished floor.   A thrashing must have
been the punishment of that dirty pitcher.

XVI

Men possess the divine power of opening all doors.
I by myself am only able to open a few.   Doors are
great fetishes which do not readily obey dogs.

XVII

The life of a dog is full of danger.   If he would
escape suffering he must be ever on the watch, during
meals and even during sleep.

XVIII

It is impossible to know whether one has acted
well towards men.   One must worship them without seeking to understand them.   Their wisdom is
mysterious.

XIX

Invocation.   O Fear, Fear august and maternal,
Fear sacred and salutary, possess me, in danger fill
me, in order that I may avoid that which is harmful,

lest, casting myself upon the enemy, I suffer for my imprudence.

XX

Vehicles there are which horses pull through the street. They are terrible. Other vehicles there are which move of themselves breathing loudly. These are also fearful. Men in rags are detestable, likewise such as carry baskets on their heads or roll casks. I do not love children who utter loud cries and flee from and pursue each other swiftly in the streets. The world is full of hostile and dreadful things.

THE NECKTIE

TO MADAME FÉLIX DECORI

THE NECKTIE

ONSIEUR BERGERET was hammer-
ing nails into the wall of his new flat.
Becoming aware that he was en-
joying the work, he began to wonder
why it gave him pleasure to knock
nails into the wall. He found the reason and lost the
pleasure. For the pleasure had consisted in hammer-
ing the nails without thinking of the reason of anything. Then, as he hung his father's portrait
in the place of honour in the drawing-room, he
meditated on the sorrows of a philosophical mind.

" It tips forward too much," said Zoé.

" Do you think so ? "

" I am sure of it. It looks as if it were going to
fall."

Monsieur Bergeret shortened the cord from which
the picture hung.

" It isn't straight," said Mademoiselle Bergeret.

" Is it not ? "

" No it hangs perceptibly too much to the left."

Monsieur Bergeret carefully readjusted it.

" And now how is it ? "

" It hangs too much to the right."

Monsieur Bergeret did his best to bring the picture-frame into line with the horizon, and then drew back three steps in order to inspect his handi-work.

" I think it is right," he said.

" It is all right now ," said Zoé. " It worries me when a picture isn't straight."

" You are not the only one whom it worries, Zoé. There are many who feel like you. Any irregularity in simple matters is irritating because it is so easy to see the difference between what is and what ought to be. Some people cannot bear to see a badly hung wall-paper. The conditions of our humanity are indeed terrible and atrocious when a crooked picture frame upsets us."

" There is nothing extraordinary in that, Lucien. Little things occupy a large place in life. You yourself are constantly interested in trifles."

" All the years that I have been gazing at this por-trait I have never remarked before what strikes me at this moment. I have just perceived that this por-trait of our father is the portrait of a young man."

"Why, of course, Lucien. When the artist

Gosselin, on his return from Rome, painted father, he was not more than thirty."

"True, sister. But when I was a boy the portrait appeared to me that of a man well on in years, and that impression clung to me. Now it has suddenly vanished. The colours of Gosselin's picture have lost their brightness; the flesh has assumed an amber tint under the varnish; the lines have grown vague, merging into shadow of an olive hue. Our father's face seems to retreat further and further into a far-distant background. But that smooth forehead, those large bright eyes, the clear pure line of the delicate cheeks, the black hair thick and shining, belong, I see it now for the first time, to a man in the flower of his youth."

"Certainly," said Zoé.

"His dress and the style of his hair are those of the old days when he was young. He wears his hair ruffled. His bottle-green coat has a high collar, he wears a nankin waistcoat and his broad black silk stock tie is wound three times round his neck."

"Ten years ago old men were still to be seen wearing ties like that," said Zoé.

"Possibly," said Monsieur Bergeret. "But it is certain that Monsieur Malorey never wore any others."

"You mean the Dean of the Faculté des Lettres

at Saint-Omer, Lucien. . . . It is thirty years and more since his death."

"He was over sixty, Zoé, when I was less than twelve—but it was then that I committed a most daring outrage on his tie."

"I think I remember that rather stupid joke," said Zoé.

"No, Zoé, you do not remember my joke. If you did you would not speak of it like that. You know that Monsieur Malorey was very particular about his personal appearance and that he was always very dignified. You remember also that he was extremely decorous. He had an old-fashioned way of speaking, which was delightful. One day when he had invited our parents to dinner for the second time he himself offered a dish of artichokes to our mother, saying : ' Just a little more of the underpart, Madame.' He was speaking according to the best traditions of politeness and of language. For our ancestors never spoke of ' the bottom of an artichoke.' But the term was antiquated and our mother had great difficulty to keep from laughing. I cannot remember, Zoé, how we came to know the artichoke story."

Zoé, who was hemming white curtains, re-plied : " We heard it because our father related it one day without noticing that we were present."

"And ever afterwards, Zoé, you could never see Monsieur Malorey without wanting to laugh."

"You laughed also."

"No, Zoé, I did not laugh at that. That which amuses other men does not make me laugh, that which amuses me does not make other men laugh. I have often noticed it. I see the ludicrous where no one else perceives it. I am gay and I am sad in the wrong places, and it has often made me look like a fool."

Monsieur Bergeret climbed a ladder in order to hang a view of Mount Vesuvius by night, during an eruption; the picture was a water-colour which he had inherited from a paternal ancestor.

"But I have not told you, sister, what I said to Monsieur Malorey."

"Lucien, while you are on the ladder, please put up the curtain-rods," said Zoé.

"I will," said her brother. "We were then living in a little house in a suburb of Saint-Omer."

"The curtain-rings are in the nail-box."

"I have them. . . . A little house with a garden."

"A very pretty garden," said Zoé. "It was

full of lilac bushes.   On the lawn was a vase
in terra cotta, at the end a maze, and a grotto
rockery, and on the wall two large blue pots.''

" Yes, Zoé, two large blue pots.   One morning,
one summer morning, Monsieur Malorey came to
our house to consult some books, that were not in
his own library and which he could not have found
in the town library, because it had been destroyed
in a fire.   My father had placed his study at the
Dean's disposal and the offer had been accepted.
It was arranged that when he had collated his texts
he would stay and lunch with us.''

" Just see if the curtains are too long, Lucien.''

" I will. . . .''

"That morning the heat was stifling.   Among
the still leaves even the birds were silent.
Sitting under a tree in the garden, I perceived in
the shaded study the back of Monsieur Malorey and
his long hair resting on the collar of his frock-coat.
Save that his hand was moving over a sheet of paper,
he did not stir.   There was nothing extraordinary
in that.   He was writing.   But what did appear to
me unusual . . .''

" Well, are they long enough ? ''

" Not by four inches, my good Zoé.''

" What, four inches ?   Show me Lucien.''

" Look. . . . What did appear to me unusual was to see Monsieur Malorey's tie on the window-sill.   Overcome by the heat, the Dean had unwound the black cravat that three times encircled his neck. And the long piece of black silk hung from side to side out of the open window.   I was seized with an uncontrollable desire to take it.   I crept softly up to the wall of the house, I stretched my arm towards the tie, I pulled it ; nothing stirred in the study ; I pulled it again ; there it was in my hand ; I went and hid it in one of the large blue pots in the garden."

" It was not a very brilliant joke, Lucien."

" No. . . I hid it in one of the large blue pots and I took care to cover it with leaves and moss. Monsieur Malorey continued for some time at work in the study.   I watched his motionless back and the long white hair flowing over the collar of his frock-coat.   Then the servant called me to lunch. As I entered the dining-room the most unexpected sight met my gaze.   Between our father and mother I saw Monsieur Malorey grave, calm, but without his necktie.   He had all his usual dignity.   He was even august.   But he was not wearing his tie.   This filled me with surprise.   I knew he could not be wearing it, since it was in the blue pot.   And yet I was prodigiously astonished to see him without it.

" I cannot think, Madame," he said softly to our mother. . . . She interrupted him : " My husband will lend you one, dear sir."

" And I reflected : ' I hid it in jest, he failed to find it in earnest.' But I was astonished."

THE MONTIL MANŒUVRES

TO OCTAVE MIRBEAU

THE MONTIL MANŒUVRES

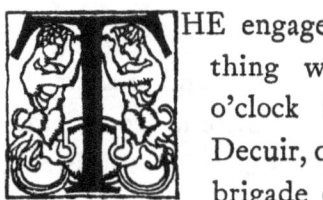HE engagement had begun; everything was going well. At ten o'clock in the morning General Decuir, of the southern army, whose brigade occupied a strong position beneath the woods of Saint-Colomban, effected a brilliant reconnaissance which demonstrated the absence of the enemy. Then the soldiers broke their fast, and the General, leaving his escort at Saint-Luchaire, drove, accompanied by Captain Varnot, in the motor-car which had come to fetch him, to the Château de Montil, where the Baronne de Bonmont had invited him to lunch. The village of Montil was hung with flags. At the entrance to the park, the General passed beneath a triumphal arch erected in his honour and decorated with flags, trophies and branches of oak interwoven with boughs of laurel.

On the steps of her castle the Baronne de Bonmont received the General and led him into a vast hall hung with weapons and glittering with steel.

" Your residence is superb, Madame, and the country is beautiful," said the General. " I have often been to shoot about here, chiefly with the Brécés, where I had the pleasure of meeting your son, if I am not mistaken."

" No, you are not mistaken," said Ernest de Bonmont, who had driven the General from Saint-Luchaire. " And to say one is bored at the Brécés is to put it mildly ! "

It was a small luncheon party. Besides the General, the Captain, the Baronne and her son, there were only Madame Worms-Clavelin and Joseph Lacrisse.

" You must take things as you find them ! " said Madame de Bonmont placing the General on her right at a table decorated with flowers over which towered an equestrian statue of Napoleon in Sèvres porcelain.

At a glance the General took in the long gallery hung with the finest Van Orley tapestries.

" You have plenty of room here ! "

" The General might have brought his brigade," said the Captain.

" I should have been delighted to receive it," replied the Baronne smiling.

The talk was simple, quiet and cordial, Every one had the good taste to avoid politics. The General was a royalist. He did not say so, but it was well known. His manners were perfect. His two sons had been arrested for crying: "Panama!" on the boulevards when President Loubet came into office. The General's own attitude had always been discreet. Horses and cannon were the topics of conversation.

"The new 75 is a gem," said the General.

"One cannot too highly commend the ease with which the firing is regulated. It is really wonderful," added Captain Varnot.

"And during the manœuvres," said Madame Worms-Clavelin, "by a new and ingenious arrangement the covers of the ammunition wagons serve as a shelter for the gunners."

Madame la Préfète was congratulated on her military knowledge.

Madame Worms-Clavelin appeared to equal advantage when she spoke of Notre-Dame des Belles-Feuilles.

"You know, General, that in this department, no further away than Brécé, we have a miraculous statue of the Blessed Virgin."

"I have heard of it," replied the General.

"Before he was made a Bishop," continued

Madame Worms-Clavelin, "the Abbé Guitrel was greatly interested in the apparitions of Notre-Dame des Belles-Feuilles. He even wrote a little book to prove that Notre-Dame des Belles-Feuilles is the special protectress of the French army."

"Tell me where I can procure a copy and I will read it," said the General.

Madame Worms-Clavelin promised to send him the book.

In short throughout the meal not a word was uttered that could be called offensive or tending to the malicious. After lunch, there was a walk in the park. Then Captain Varnot took his leave.

"Let my escort wait for me at Saint-Luchaire, Captain," said the General. And turning to Lacrisse, he said:

"Manœuvres are a picture of war, but they are not a true picture because everything is thought out and planned whereas in war it is the unexpected that happens."

"Will you come and see the pheasantry, General?" said Madame de Bonmont.

"With pleasure, Madame."

She turned round.

"Are you not coming, Ernest?"

Ernest had been stopped on his way by the worthy Raulin, mayor of Montil.

" Excuse me, Baron," he was saying. " But if you could say a word to General Decuir for me, if only the artillery would pass over St. John's Hill, across my lucerne field."

" What ! Haven't you a good crop, Raulin ? Is that why you want it trampled on ? "

" Not at all, not at all. The crop is excellent, Baron ; the harvest next month promises to be good. But compensation is good also. Last time it was Houssiaux who had it. Isn't it my turn now ? I am mayor, I bear all the burdens of the commune, is it not fair therefore that when there is any bonus to be given. . . . ? "

The General was taken to the pheasantry.

" It is time," he said, " that I rejoined my brigade."

" Oh ! You will reach it in no time with my thirty horse-power," said the young baron.

They inspected the kennels, the stables and the gardens.

" Your roses are superb," said the General, who was fond of flowers. Through the perfumed air there boomed the sound of cannon.

" It has a festal sound and uplifts the heart,"
said Lacrisse.

" Like the sound of bells," said Madame Worms-
Clavelin.

" You are a true Frenchwoman, Madame," said
the General. " Every word you utter breathes the
purest patriotism."

It was four o'clock. The General could not stay
a minute longer. Fortunately in " the thirty
horse-power " he would reach his brigade in no
time.

With the young baron, Lacrisse and the chauffeur
he entered the car, and once again passed beneath
his triumphal arch.

In forty minutes he was at Saint-Luchaire. But
his escort was not there. In vain the four motorists
looked for Captain Varnot. The village was deserted. Not a soldier to be found. A butcher was
passing in his cart. They asked him where Decuir's
division was : he replied :

" Try the Cagny road. Just now I heard firing
in the direction of Cagny, and it was loud too, I can
assure you."

" Cagny, where is that ? " inquired the General.

" Don't you trouble, I know," said the Baron.
" I will drive you there."

And, as the drive would be a long one, he gave the General a dust-coat, a cap and goggles.

They started on the departmental road; they passed Saint-André, Villeneuve, Letaf, Saint-Porçain, Truphême, Mirange, and they saw the Cagny pond shining like brass in the light of the setting sun. On the high-road, they met dragoons of the northern army who knew nothing of the whereabouts of the Decuir brigade, but they maintained that the southern army was engaged at Saint-Paulain.

Saint-Paulain was forty-five kilometres distant, in the direction of Montil.

The car turned round, went back down the departmental road, returned through Mirange, Truphême, Saint-Porçain, Letaf, Villeneuve and Saint-André.

"Put on more speed," ordered the Baron.

And the car passed through the streets of Verry-les-Fougerais, Suttières and Rary-la-Vicomté, raising a cloud of dust golden like a glory and crushing pigs and poultry. Two kilometres from Saint-Paulain, they came on the outposts of the southern army holding La Saulaie, Mesville and Le Sourdais. There they learned that the whole of the northern army was on the other side of the Ilette.

H

They drove towards Torcy-la-Mirande in order to strike the river by the heights of Vieux-Bac.

When in the course of an hour they began to perceive by the evening light a sheet of white mist hanging over the low lying meadows:

" Gad," said the young Baron, " we can't cross: the Ilette Bridge is destroyed."

" What ! " exclaimed the General, " the Ilette Bridge destroyed ? What's that you say ? The Bridge destroyed ! "

" Why, General! yes. In the plan of the manœuvres the Bridge is destroyed in theory."

The General did not appreciate the joke.

" I admire your wit young man," he said sharply.

At Vieux-Bac they thundered across the iron bridge and followed the ancient Roman road, which connects Torcy-la-Mirande with the chief town of the department. In the sky, Venus was kindling her silver flame close by the crescent moon. They travelled about thirty kilometres without meeting any troops. At Saint-Évariste there was a terrible hill to climb. The car groaned like a tired beast, but did not stop. Coming down it went over some stones and was on the point of capsizing in a ditch. Then the road was excellent as far as

Mallemanche, where they arrived at night, during a surprise.

The sky was glittering with stars. Trumpets were sounding. Lanterns were casting a yellow gleam on the blue road. Foot soldiers were pillaging the houses. The inhabitants were at the windows.

" Although merely theoretical it is all extremely impressive," said Lacrisse.

The General was told that his brigade was in possession of Villeneuve on the left wing of the victorious army. The enemy was in full retreat.

Villeneuve is at the junction of the Ilette and the Claine, twenty kilometres from Mallemanche.

" We must make for Villeneuve ! " said the General. " At last we know what we have to do, and a good thing too."

The Villeneuve road was so encumbered with artillery, ammunition wagons and gunners asleep and wrapped in their great cloaks, that it was very difficult for the car to thread its way. A canteen-woman sitting in a cart decorated with Chinese lanterns hailed the motorists and offered them coffee and liqueurs.

" We won't say no," replied the General.

"We have swallowed dust enough during the manœuvres."

"They drank a liqueur and pressed on to Villeneuve, which was occupied by the infantry.

"But where is my brigade ?" cried the General, who was growing anxious.

They questioned eagerly all the officers they met. But no one could give them news of the Decuir brigade.

"What ! no news ? Then it is not at Villeneuve ? Incredible !"

"Gentlemen," they heard in a woman's voice, shrill and bell-like. They looked up and beheld a head studded with curl-papers; it belonged to the postmistress.

"Gentlemen, there are two Villeneuves. This is Villeneuve-sur-Claine. Perhaps it is Villeneuve-la-Bataille that you want.

"Perhaps," said the Baron.

"That is a long way off," said the postmistress. You must go first to Montil. . . . Do you know Montil ?"

"Yes," replied the Baron, "we know Montil."

"Then you go on to Saint-Michel-du-Mont ; you take the main road and . . . ."

From the window of a neighbouring house with

gilded scutcheons came out a head wrapped in a comforter :

" Gentlemen . . . ."

And the notary of Villeneuve-sur-Claine gave his advice :

" To reach Villeneuve-la-Bataille, you would do better to cross through the Forest of Tongues. . . . You go to La Croix du Perron, you turn to the right . . ."

" That's enough. I know the Forest of Tongues," said the Baron, " I have hunted there with the Brécés. . . . Thank you, sir. . . . Thank you, Mademoiselle."

" Don't mention it," said the postmistress.

" At your service, gentlemen," said the notary.

" What if we went to the inn and had a cocktail ? " said the Baron.

" I should like something to eat," said Lacrisse. " I am done up."

" Courage, gentlemen," said the General.   " We will make up for it at Villeneuve-la-Bataille."

And they started.   They passed through Vély, La Roche, Les Saules, Meulette, La Taillerie and entered the Forest of Tremble.   A dazzling light ran before them into the shades of night and of the forest.   They reached La Croix-du-Perron, then the

Roi-Henri cross-roads. They fled wildly through the silence and solitude. They saw the deer glide by and the lights in the charcoal-burners' huts. Suddenly in a deep cutting the ominous noise of an explosion made them shudder. The car skidded and knocked up against a tree.

" What is the matter ? " asked the General, who had been thrown head over heels.

Lacrisse groaned ; he was lying on a bed of fern.

But Ernest, lantern in hand, was saying dismally :

" The tyre has burst. . . . But worse than that the front wheel is twisted."

ÉMILE

ÉMILE

ADEMOISELLE BERGERET was silent. She smiled, which was unusual.

"Why are you laughing, Zoé ? " asked Monsieur Bergeret.

" I was thinking of Émile Vincent."

" What Zoé ! You can think of that excellent man, whom we have just lost, whom we loved and whom we mourn, and you can laugh ! "

" I laugh because I can see him again as he used to be, and the old memories are the strongest. But you should know, Lucien, that all smiles are not joyful any more than all tears are sorrowful. It takes an old maid to explain that."

" I am not unaware, Zoé, that laughter is the result of nervous agitation. Madame de Custine as she bade adieu in the prison to her husband condemned to death by the Revolutionary Tribunal, was seized with a fit of uncontrollable laughter at the sight of a prisoner walking past her in dressing-gown and night-cap, with his face painted and a candle in his hand."

" That is not at all the same thing," said Zoé.

" No," replied Monsieur Bergeret.   " But I re-member what happened to me when I heard of the death of poor Demay who used to sing comic songs at the cafés concerts.   It was one evening during a reception at the Prefecture.   Worms-Clavelin said : ' Demay is dead.'

" I for my part received the tidings in decorous sadness.   And, reflecting that never again should I hear that wondrous woman sing : *Je cas' des noisett's en m'asseyant d'ssus,** I tasted to the dregs all the melancholy the thought engendered.   I let it drip into my soul and relapsed into silence.   The Chief Secretary, Monsieur Lacarelle, exclaimed in his deep voice, through his military moustache : ' De-may dead !   What a loss to the gaiety of France ! ' ' It was in the evening paper,' said Judge Pilloux. ' True,' added General Cartier de Chalmont gently, ' and I am informed that she died consoled by the rites of the Church.'

" At the General's simple words suddenly a strange, incongruous vision flashed before my eyes. I imagined the end of the world as it is

* I crack nuts by sitting on them.

described in the 'Dies Irae,' according to the testimony of David and the Sibyl. I beheld the age reduced to ashes; I saw the dead issuing forth from their tombs, and, at the angel's summons, crowding before the Judgment Seat, and the massive Demay mother-naked at the Lord's right hand. At this conception I burst out laughing in the presence of the astonished officials civil and military. But worse still, the vision obsessed me and I added between bursts of laughter : ' You will see that by her very presence, she will upset the solemnity of the Last Judgment.' Never, Zoé, were words less comprehensible, less relevant."

"You are absurd, Lucien. I never have those curious visions. I smiled because I imagined our poor friend Vincent just as he was in life. That was all. It was quite natural. I mourn for him with all my heart. We never had a better friend."

"I too was very fond of him, Zoé, and I too when I think of him am tempted to smile. It was strange how so much military ardour came to reside in so small a body and how a soul so heroic could dwell in a form so spruce and plump. His life passed quietly in the suburb of a provincial town. He was a brushmaker at Les Tintelleries. But there was room in his heart for something besides his business."

" He was even smaller than Uncle Jean," said Mademoiselle Bergeret.

" And he was martial, he was civic, he was imperial," said Monsieur Bergeret.

" He was a very excellent man," said Mademoiselle Bergeret.

" He was in the war of 1870, Zoé.   In that year he was twenty.   I was only twelve.   He seemed to me old and full of years.   One day in the Terrible Year, he entered our peaceful provincial dwelling with the clashing of steel.   He came to bid us farewell.   He was dressed in the startling uniform of a *franc-tireur*.   Protruding from his scarlet belt were the butts of two horse-pistols.   And because a smile must enter even into the most tragic moments, the unconscious humour of some unknown armourer had hitched him to an enormous cavalry sword. Do not blame me for the expression, Zoé ; it occurs in one of Cicero's letters.   ' Whoever,' says the orator, ' hitched my son-in-law to that sword ? '

" What astonished me most in the equipment of our friend Émile Vincent was this huge sword. To my childish mind it seemed to augur victory. You, Zoé, I believed, were more impressed by his

boots, for you looked up from your work and cried :
' Why it is Puss in Boots ! ' "

"Did I say ' Puss in Boots.'   Poor Émile."

"You said ' Puss in Boots '; and you need not
regret it, Zoé.   Madame d'Abrantès in her
Memoirs relates how a young girl seeing Napoleon,
then young and slender, ridiculously accoutred as
a General of the Republic, likewise called him ' Puss
in Boots.'   Bonaparte never forgave her for it.
Our friend was more magnanimous ; the title did
not offend him.   Émile Vincent and his company
were placed under the command of a general who
did not like *francs-tireurs*, and who thus harangued
them: ' It is not everything to be dressed for
a carnival.   You must know how to fight.'

"The caustic speech did not trouble my friend
Vincent.   He was splendid throughout the campaign.   One day he was seen to approach the
enemy's outposts with all the calm of a short-
sighted man and a hero.   He could not see three
steps before him.   Nothing could make him retreat.   For the remaining thirty years of his life,
while he was making carpet-brooms, he lived on the
memory of that campaign.   He read military news-
papers, presided over meetings of his former companions in arms, was present at the unveiling of

monuments raised to the soldiers of 1870. When from time to time there were erected on French soil monuments to Vercingetorix, to Jeanne d'Arc, to the soldiers of the Loire, at the head of the workmen in his factory, Émile defiled before them. He made patriotic speeches. And, here Zoé, we approach a scene in the comedy of life, the melancholy humour of which may one day be appreciated. During the Dreyfus Affair it occurred to Émile Vincent to say that Esterhazy was a fraud and a traitor. He said it because he knew it was so and because he was far too candid ever to conceal the truth. From that day he was regarded as the enemy of his country and of the army. He was treated as a traitor and an alien. He suffered from heart disease, and his grief at this treatment aggravated the malady. He died of sorrow and of shock. The last time I saw him he was talking of military tactics and strategy. They were his favourite topic of conversation. Although the campaign of '70, in which he had served, was conducted with the greatest disorder and confusion, he was persuaded that the art of war is the finest of all arts. And I fear that I must have vexed him by saying that properly speaking there is no art of war, for the arts that are really employed in campaigns are those of peace ; baking, farriery, the maintenance of order, chemistry, etc."

" Why did you say such things, Lucien ? " asked Mademoiselle Bergeret.

" Because I was convinced of their truth," replied her brother. " What is called strategy is really the art practised by Cook's agency. It consists in crossing rivers by way of bridges and getting the other side of mountains through passes. As for military tactics, the rules are childish. Great Captains pay no attention to them. Although they would never admit it, they leave much to chance. Their art is to create prejudices in their favour. Conquest becomes easy to them when they are believed to be unconquerable. It is only on a plan that a battle assumes that aspect of order and regularity which reveals a dominant will."

" Poor Émile Vincent ! " sighed Mademoiselle Bergeret. " He was indeed passionately fond of the army. And I agree with you that he must have suffered cruelly when he found military society treating him as an enemy. General Cartier de Chalmot's wife was very hard on him. She knew better than anyone that he subscribed largely to military charities. And yet she would have nothing to do with him when she heard that he had called

Esterhazy a fraud and a traitor. She broke with him in the most undisguised fashion. One day when he came to her house, she went close up to the hall where he was waiting and exclaimed so that he might hear her: 'Tell him that I am not at home.' Nevertheless she is not a malicious woman."

"No certainly," replied Monsieur Bergeret. "She acted according to that holy simplicity of which still better examples may be found in earlier times. Only commonplace virtues are left to us nowadays. And poor Émile died of nothing but grief."

ADRIENNE BUQUET

TO DR. GEORGES DUMAS

ADRIENNE BUQUET

E were finishing our dinner at the tavern when Laboullée said to me :

"I admit that second-sight, hypnotic suggestion from a distance, presentiments subsequently fulfilled, all those phenomena dependent on a condition of the organism at present ill-defined, are not for the most part proved in such a manner as to satisfy the demands of scientific criticism. They nearly all rest on evidence which, though genuine, permits of some uncertainty as to the nature of the phenomena. That the facts about them are vague, I admit. But that they are possible I cannot doubt since I myself have witnessed one. By a happy chance I was myself enabled to make the minutest scrutiny. You may believe me when I tell you that I proceeded methodically and that I was careful to eliminate every possibility of error."

As he uttered this sentence, the young doctor with both hands smote his hollow chest padded with

pamphlets and inclined towards me across the table
his bald head with its projecting forehead.

" Yes, my good fellow," he added, " by a wonderful stroke of luck one of those phonomena described
by Myers and Podmore as ' phantoms of the living '
took place in all its phases before the very eyes of a
man of science. I observed everything and noted
everything down."

" I am listening."

" The time of the occurrence," resumed Laboullée,
" was the summer of '91. My friend, Paul Buquet,
of whom I have often spoken to you, was then living
with his wife in a little flat in the Rue de Grenelle,
opposite the fountain. You did not know Buquet ? "

" I have seen him two or three times. A big
fellow, bearded up to the eyes. His wife was dark,
pale, large featured with long grey eyes."

" Exactly : a bilious temperament, nervous but
fairly well balanced. However, when a woman lives
in Paris her nerves get the upper hand and—then
the deuce is in it. Did you ever see Adrienne ? "

" I met her one evening in the Rue de la Paix,
standing with her husband in front of a jeweller's
window, her eyes fixed on some sapphires. A good-
looking woman and deucedly well dressed for the
wife of a poor wretch buried in the cellars of a

manufacturing chemist. Buquet was never success-
ful, was he ?

" For five years Buquet had been working for the
firm of Jacob, manufacturers of photographic
materials and apparatus in the Boulevard Magenta.
From day to day he expected to be made a partner.
Although he did not earn his thousands, he had a
fairly good position. His prospects were not bad.
He was a patient, simple fellow and hard working.
He was the kind to succeed in the long run. Meanwhile his wife cost him little. Like a true Parisian,
she was an excellent manager, for ever making
wonderful bargains in linen, frocks, laces and jewels.
She astonished her husband by her cleverness in
dressing extremely well on nothing at all and Paul
was gratified to see her always looking so nice and
wearing such elegant under-linen. But these details
cannot interest you."

" My dear Laboullée, I am very interested."

" At any rate all this chatter is beside the point.
As you know I was Paul Buquet's schoolfellow. We
knew each other in the second class at Louis-le-
Grand ; and we had not lost sight of one another
when, at the age of twenty-six, before he had made
his position, he married Adrienne for love, and
with nothing but what she stood up in, as we say.

Our friendship did not cease with his marriage. Rather, Adrienne was kind to me, and I used often to dine with the young couple. As you know, I am doctor to the actor Laroche; I mix with theatrical folk, who from time to time give me tickets: Adrienne and her husband were very fond of the theatre. When I had a box for the evening I used to go and dine with them and take them afterwards to the Comédie-Française. At dinner time I was always sure to find Buquet, who came home from his factory regularly at half-past six, his wife and their friend Géraud."

" Géraud," I inquired, " Marcel Géraud who was in a bank and who used to wear such beautiful ties ? "

" The very same. He was a constant visitor at the house. Being a confirmed bachelor and sociable, he dined there every day. He used to bring lobsters, *pâtés* and all kinds of dainties. He was pleasant, amiable and taciturn. Buquet could not get along without him, and we used to take him to the theatre."

" How old was he ? "

" Géraud ? I don't know. Between thirty and forty. . . . One day when Laroche had given me a box, I went as usual to the Rue de Grenelle, to my friends, the Buquets. I was rather late, and when I arrived dinner was ready. Paul was complaining of being hungry ; but Adrienne could not make up her mind to sit down to table in Géraud's absence. ' My children,' I cried, ' I have a box in the second row for the Français ! They are playing " Denise " ! ' ' Come,' said Buquet, ' let us have dinner quickly and try not to miss the first act.' The servant put dinner on the table. Adrienne seemed anxious, and it was evident that she turned against every mouthful. Buquet was noisily swallowing vermicelli, catching the threads hanging from his moustache with his tongue. ' Women are extraordinary,' he exclaimed. ' Just fancy, Laboullée, Adrienne is anxious because Géraud has not come to dinner this evening. She imagines all manner of things. Tell her how absurd she is. Géraud may have been detained. He has his business. He is a bachelor ; no one has a right to ask him how he spends his time. What surprises me is that he should devote nearly all his evenings to us. It is very good of him. The least we can do is to leave him some liberty. My principle is never to worry about what my friends are doing. But women are different.' Madame Buquet in a trembling voice rejoined : ' I am anxious. I fear something may have happened to Monsieur Géraud.' Meanwhile Buquet was hurrying on the meal. 'Sophie!' he called to the servant, 'bring in the beef, the salad! Sophie! the cheese! the coffee.' I observed that Madame Buquet had eaten nothing. 'Come,' said her husband, 'go and dress; and don't make us lose the first act. A play by Dumas is very different from an operetta of which all you want is to catch an air or two. Every play of Dumas' is a series of logical deductions, not one of which must be lost. Go, my love; as for me I have only to put on my frock-coat.' She rose, and slowly, as if almost against her will, passed into her room.

" We drank our coffee, her husband and I, smoking our cigarettes. 'That good Géraud,' said Paul, 'I am vexed all the same that he isn't here this evening. He would have been glad to see " Denise." But can you understand Adrienne's worrying over his absence? I have tried in vain to make her understand that the good fellow may have business which he does not confide to us. Who can tell? Why it may be a love affair! She won't understand. Give me a cigarette.' Just as I was handing him my case, we heard proceeding from the next room a long cry of terror followed by a dull bumpish thud, the sound of something falling. 'Adrienne!'

cried Buquet. And he rushed into the bedroom.
I followed. We found Adrienne lying full length
on the floor, motionless, her face white and her eyes
turned up. There was no epileptic or kindred
symptom, no foam on the lips. The limbs were
extended but not rigid. The pulse was rapid and
unequal. I helped her husband to put her into an
arm-chair. Almost immediately her circulation was
restored ; the blood rushed to her face, which was
generally of a dull white. ' There,' she said, point-
ing to her wardrobe mirror, 'there! I saw him
there. As I was fastening my bodice, I saw him in
the glass. I turned round, thinking he was behind
me. But seeing no one I understood and fell.'

" Meanwhile I was trying to asce tain whether she
had sustained any injury from her fall and I found
none. Buquet was giving her sugared *eau des carmes.*
' Come, my love,' he was saying, 'gather yourself
together! Who was it you saw ? What do you say ? '
She turned white again. ' Oh! I saw him, him,
Marcel.' 'She saw Géraud! that is odd,' cried
Buquet. ' Yes, I saw him,' she resumed gravely:
' he looked at me without speaking, like that.'
And she assumed a haggard look. Buquet turned
towards me wonderingly. ' Don't be anxious,'
I replied, ' such illusions are not serious, they may

proceed from indigestion. We will consider the matter at leisure. For the moment we may put it on one side. At La Charité I know a patient suffering from gastric disease who used to see cats under all the furniture.'

"In a few minutes Madame Buquet having completely recovered, her husband took out his watch and said: 'If you think that the theatre will not do her any harm, Laboullée, it is time we started. I will tell Sophie to go for a cab.' Adrienne quickly put on her hat. 'Paul! Paul! Doctor! do listen: let us go to Monsieur Géraud's first. I am anxious, more anxious than I can tell you.'

"'You are mad!' cried Buquet. 'Whatever do you imagine is wrong with Géraud? We saw him yesterday in perfect health.'

"She gave me a look so imploring that the burning intensity of it went straight to my heart. 'Laboullée, my friend, let us go at once to Monsieur Géraud's.'

"I could not refuse her, she asked so entreatingly. Paul was grumbling: he wanted to see the first act. I said to him: 'We had better go to Geraud's, it will not take us far out of our way.' The cab was waiting for us. I called to the driver: '5 Rue du Louvre. And as quick as you can.'

"Géraud lived at number 5 Rue du Louvre, not far from his bank, in a little three-roomed flat filled with neckties. They were the good fellow's weakness. Barely had we stopped at the door when Buquet leaped from the cab and looking in at the porter's lodge, asked: 'How is Monsieur Géraud?' The *concierge* replied: 'Monsieur Géraud returned at five o'clock and took his letters. He has not gone out since. If you want to see him, it is the back staircase, on the fourth floor, to the right.' But Buquet was already at the cab door, crying: 'Géraud is at home. You see, my love, how absurd you were. To the Comédie Française, driver.' Then Adrienne almost threw herself out of the cab. 'Paul, I implore you, go up to Gér ud's. See him. See him, you must.'

"'Go up four flights!' he said, shrugging his shoulders. 'Adrienne you will make us miss the play. Really, when a woman once gets an idea into her head. . . .'

"I remained alone in the cab with Madame Buquet, and I saw her eyes turned towards the house door and gleaming in the darkness. At length Paul returned: 'Well,' he said, 'I rang three times and without an answer. After all, my love, he must have had his reasons for not wishing to be disturbed.

He may be with a woman.   There would be nothing
astonishing in that.'   Adrienne's look became so
tragic, that I myself felt anxious.   When I came to
think of it, it was unnatural for Géraud, who never
dined at home, to remain up there from five o'clock
in the afternoon until half-past seven.   'Wait here
for me,' I said to Monsieur and Madame Buquet,
' I will go and speak to the *concierge*.'   The woman
also thought it strange that Géraud should not have
gone out to dinner as usual.   It was she who waited
on the fourth-floor tenant, so she had the key of the
flat.   She took it down from the rack and offered
to go up with me.   When we had reached the land-
ing, she opened the door, and from the vestibule
called three or four times : ' Monsieur Géraud ! '
Receiving no reply, she ventured to enter the first
room which was the bedroom.   Again she called :
' Monsieur Géraud ! Monsieur Géraud ! '   No
reply.   It was quite dark.   We had no matches.
' There must be a box of Swedish matches on the
table de nuit,' the woman said, beginning to tremble
and afraid to move.   I began to feel on the table
and my fingers came in contact with a sticky sub-
stance.   ' There is no mistake about that,' I
thought, ' It is blood.'

    "When at length we had lit a candle, we saw

Géraud stretched on his bed, with a wound in his head. His arm was hanging down on to he carpet where his revolver had fallen. A letter ned with blood was open on the table. It was i his hand-writing and addressed to Monsieur and Madame Buquet. It began thus: ' My dear friends, you have been the charm and joy of my life.' It went on to tell them of his resolve to die without clearly explaining for what reason, but he hinted that financial embarrassment was the cause of his suicide. I perceived that death had taken place about an hour ago. So that he had killed himself at the very moment when Madame Buquet had seen him in the glass.

"Now is not this just what I was telling you, a perfectly authentic case of second sight, or to use a more exact term an instance of that curious psychical synchronism which science is studying to-day with a zeal which far surpasses its success."

" It may be something quite different," I replied. " Are you quite sure that there was nothing between Marcel Géraud and Madame Buquet ? "

" Why ? . . . I never noticed anything. And after all, what would that prove ? . . ."

THE INTAGLIO

THE INTAGLIO

HAD come to him at noon by invitation. We lunched in the dining-room long as a church nave, a veritable treasure-house filled with the ancient gold and silver work he has collected. I found him not exactly sad but meditative. His conversation now and again suggested the light and graceful turn of his wit. An occasional word revealed the rare delicacy of his artistic tastes and his passion for sport, by no means allayed by a terrible fall from his horse which had split his head open. But constantly the flow of his ideas was checked as if they had been barred by some obstacle.

From this conversation, which was somewhat fatiguing to follow, all I retain is that he had just sent a couple of white peacocks to his chateau of Raray and that without any special reason he had for three weeks been neglecting his friends, forsaking even the most intimate, Monsieur and Madame N.

It was plain enough to me that he had not asked

me to come and listen to confidences such as those. While we were taking our coffee, I asked him what it was he had to tell me. He looked at me rather surprised :

" Had I anything to tell you ? "

" *Dame !* You wrote: ' Come and lunch tomorrow. I want to talk to you.' "

As he was silent I took the letter from my pocket and showed it to him. The address was in his attractive running hand, somewhat irregular. On the envelope there was a seal in violet wax.

He passed his hand over his forehead.

" I remember. Be so kind as to go to Féral's, he will show you a study by Romney ; a young woman ; golden hair the reflection of which gilds her cheeks and forehead. . . . Pupils dark blue, giving a bluish tinge to the whole eye. . . . The warm freshness of her complexion. . . . It is delicious. And an arm like gold-beater's skin. However, look at it and see if. . . ."

He paused. And with his hand on the door handle :

" Wait for me. I will put on my coat and we will go out together."

Left alone in the dining-room, I went to the window, and, more attentively than before, examined the seal of violet wax. It bore the imprint of an antique intaglio, representing a satyr raising the veil of a nymph who was asleep at the foot of a pillar, under a laurel-tree. During the best Roman period the subject was a favourite one with painters and with engravers of precious stones. This representation appeared to me excellent. The purity of the style, the perfect feeling for form, the harmonious grouping, converted this scene no longer than one's finger-nail, into a composition vast and imposing.

I was under the spell when my friend appeared through the half-open door.

" Come, let's be off," he said.

He had his hat on and seemed to be in a hurry to go out.

I congratulated him on his seal.

" I was not aware that you possessed this beautiful gem."

He replied that he had not had it long, only about six weeks. It was a find. He took it from the finger on which he wore it set in a ring, and put it in my hand.

It is well known that stones engraved in this fine classic style are generally cornelians. I was somewhat surprised therefore to see a dull gem, of a dark violet.

" What ! " I cried, " an amethyst."

" Yes, a melancholy stone and unlucky. Do you think it is a genuine antique ? "

He called for a magnifying glass. And now I was better able to admire the carving of the intaglio. It was obviously a masterpiece of Greek glyptography dating from the early Empire. Among all the precious stones in the Museum at Naples I had never seen anything more beautiful. With the glass it was possible to distinguish on the pillar an emblem often found on monuments dedicated to some subject of the Bacchic cycle. I pointed it out to him.

He shrugged his shoulders and smiled. The gem was in an open setting. It occurred to me to examine the reverse ; and I was very surprised to find thereon an inscription of a clumsy crudity dating evidently from a period much less remote than that of the intaglio. In a measure these signs resembled the engraving on those Abraxas stones * so familiar to antiquaries. In spite of my inexperience I believed them to be magic signs. That was also my friend's opinion.

* Stones so called because they bore the mystic words Abraxas, Abrasax, known also as Basilidian stones because they were the symbol of the Basilidians, a gnostic sect.

" It is thought," he said, " to be a cabalistic formula, imprecations taken from a Greek poet..."

" Which poet ? "

" I am not very well up in them."

" Theocritus."

" Theocritus perhaps."

Through the glass I could make out distinctly a group of four letters :

K H P H

" That doesn't spell a name," said my friend.

" I pointed out to him that in Greek it is the equivalent of :

K E R E

And I gave him back the stone. He looked at it long in a dazed manner and then put it on to his finger.

" Come," he said briskly. " Come."

" Where are you going ? "

" Towards the Madeleine. And you ? "

" I ? Where am I going ? *Parbleu !* I am going to Gaulot's to see a horse which he refuses to buy until I have looked at it. For, as you know, I am an authority on horses and something of a veterinary surgeon to boot. I may describe myself also as a furniture broker, an upholsterer, an architect, a

gardener, and if need be a stock-jobber. Ah! my
friend if only I had the energy I would cut out all
the Jews."

We went out into the *faubourg ;* and, as we walked
my friend assumed a gait very different from his
habitual nonchalance. His pace soon became so
rapid that I had difficulty in keeping up with him.
In front of us was a woman rather well dressed. He
called my attention to her.

" Her back is round, and she is heavy of figure.
But look at her ankle. I am sure the leg is charming.
Have you not noticed that the build of horses, of
women, and of all fine animals is very much the same ?
Coarse and large in the fleshy parts, their limbs
become thin towards the joints, where they display
the fineness of the bones. Look at that woman ;
above her waist she is not worth a glance. But her
limbs ! How free, how powerful ! How well
balanced the movement of her walk ! And how
fine the leg just above the ankle ! And the thigh I
am sure is nervously supple and really beautiful."

Then he added with that acquired wisdom which
he was ever ready to communicate :

" You must not ask everything from one woman ;
you must take beauty where you find it. It is
deucedly rare, is beauty ! "

Whereupon, through a mysterious association of ideas, he raised his left hand and looked at his intaglio. I said to him:

" Then have you abandoned your little armorial tree and taken as your crest that marvellous Bacchante ? "

" Ah ! Yes, the beech, the *fau* of Du Fau. In Poitou, under Louis XVI, my great grandfather was what was then called a nobleman, that is he was an ennobled commoner. Later he joined a revolutionary club at Poitiers and acquired national property, which procures for me to-day, in a society of Jews and Americans, the friendship of princes and the rank of an aristocrat. Why did I forsake the *fau* of the Du Fau ? Why ? It was worth almost as much as the *chêne* * of Duchesne de la Sicotière. And I have exchanged it for a bacchante, a barren laurel and an emblematical stone."

Just as with ironical emphasis he was uttering these words, we reached the house of his friend Gaulot ; but Du Fau passed the two copper knockers representing Neptune, gleaming on the door like bath taps.

" I thought you were so eager to go and see Gaulot ? "

* Oak.

He appeared not to hear me and quickened his step. He continued breathlessly as far as the Rue Matignon, down which he turned. Then suddenly he stopped in front of a tall, melancholy, five-storied house. In silence he looked anxiously at the flat stucco façade with its numerous windows.

" Are you going to be there long ? " I asked him. " Do you know that Madame Cère lives in this house ? "

I knew that name would annoy him. Madame Cère was a woman whose artificial beauty, well-known venality and obvious stupidity he had always detested. Old and of neglected appearance she was suspected of being a shop-lifter and appropriating lace. But in a weak almost plaintive voice, he replied :

" Do you think so ? "

" I am sure of it. Look at those windows on the second story and those hideous curtains with red leopards."

He shook his head.

" But certainly Madame Cère lives there. At this very moment she is probably behind one of those red leopards."

He seemed as if he would like to call on her. I expressed my surprise.

" Once you could not tolerate her. That was when every one considered her beautiful and ornamental; when she inspired fatal passion and tragic love you used to say : ' If it were only for the coarseness of her skin the woman would fill me with insurmountable disgust. But besides she is flat-chested and big-jointed.' Now, when all her charms have faded, have you succeeded in discovering one of those little points of beauty, with which as you were saying just now, we ought to be contented ? What do you make of the fineness of her ankle and the nobility of her heart ? A tall gawky woman without bust or hips, who, as she entered a salon, cast a sweeping gaze round the room, and by this simple trick attracted a crowd of those vain and imbecile creatures who ruin themselves for women devoid of natural charms."

I paused, rather ashamed of having spoken thus of a woman. But this woman had given such abundant proof of her revolting malice, that I could not resist the feeling of repugnance she inspired. In truth I should not have expressed myself thus, had I not been convinced of her falseness and her evil disposition. Moreover I had the satisfaction of perceiving that Du Fau had not heard a single word of what I had said.

He began to talk as if to himself.

"Whether I call on her or not it is all the same. For six weeks I have visited nowhere without meeting her. Houses, which I have not entered for many years, I now return to, why I know not! Queer houses too!"

Unable to comprehend the lure which drew him, I left him there, standing in front of the open door. That Du Fau, who had loathed Madame Cère when she was beautiful, that he, who had repulsed her advances when she was in her prime, should seek her now that she was old and a victim of drugs, must result from a deterioration which I had not expected in my friend. Such an uncommon vagary I should have declared impossible if in the obscure domain of sensual pathology one could ever be sure of anything.

A month later, I left Paris without an opportunity of again meeting Paul Du Fau. After spending a few days in Brittany, I went to stay with my cousin B—— at Trouville. Her children were there with her. The first week of my visit to the Chalet des Alcyons was spent in giving lessons in water-colours to my nieces, in teaching my nephews to fence and in hearing my cousin play Wagner.

On Sunday morning I went with the family as far
as the church, and while they were at mass I wandered
about the town. Walking along the beach road
lined with toy stalls and curiosity shops, I saw in
front of me Madame Cère. Languid, solitary and
forlorn, she was going down to the bathing-huts.
The dragging of her feet suggested that her shoes
were down at heel. Her frock, torn and crumpled,
seemed to be dropping off her body. For one
moment she looked round. Her hollow vacant eyes
and her hanging lip positively alarmed me. While
the women cast sidelong glances at her, she went on
her way dismal and indifferent.

Obviously the poor woman was poisoned with
morphia. At the end of the street she stopped
before the shop window of Madame Guillot, and,
with her long thin hand, began to feel the laces.
Her eager glance at that moment reminded me of
the tattle that circulated about her in the big shops.
The stout Madame Guillot, who was showing out
some customers, appeared at the door. And
Madame Cère, putting down the lace, resumed her
dreary walk to the beach.

" You haven't bought anything for a long time !
What a bad customer you are ! " cried Madame
Guillot as she saw me. Come, look at some buckles

and fans which the young ladies, your nieces, thought very pretty. How good looking they grow, the young ladies ! "

Then she looked at the disappearing form of Madame Cère and shook her head as if to say :

" Isn't it unfortunate ?   Eh ? "

I had to buy some paste buckles for my nieces. While my purchase was being wrapped up, through the shop window I saw Du Fau going down to the beach. He was walking very quickly with an anxious air. In the manner of agitated persons, he was biting his nails, which enabled me to observe that he wore the amethyst on his finger.

I was surprised to see him, especially as he said he was going to Dinard. He has a chalet there and harriers. When I fetched my cousin from church, I asked her whether she knew that Du Fau was at Trouville. She nodded. Then, slightly embarrassed :

" Our poor friend is quite absurd.   He is tied to that woman.   And really. . . ."

She paused and then resumed :

" It is he who pursues her.   I can't understand it."

Du Fau was indeed pursuing her.   In a few days

I had certain proof of it. I saw him constantly dogging the steps of Madame Cère and of Monsieur Cère, whom no one knows whether to regard as a stupid or an obliging husband. His dulness saves him and makes it possible to give him the benefit of the doubt. Once this woman was blindly set on attracting Du Fau, who is a useful friend in households ostentatious but not wealthy. But Du Fau made no attempt to conceal his dislike for her. He used to say in her presence: " An artificially beautiful woman is more detestable than an ugly woman. The latter may offer pleasant surprises. The other is naught but a fruit filled with ashes." On that occasion the strength of Du Fau's feeling imparted to its expression a biblical elevation of style. Now Madame Cère ignored him. Grown indifferent to men, she now cared only for her De Pravaz syringe * and her friend, the Countess V——. These two women were inseparable ; and the innocence of their friendship was thought to be rendered possible by the circumstance that they were both moribund. Nevertheless Du Fau was always with them on their excursions. One day I saw him carrying Monsieur Cère's heavy field-glasses slung over his shoulders. He persuaded Madame Cère to go out in a boat with

* A morphia syringe.

him, and the whole beach fixed its eyes upon them with an unholy glee.

Naturally enough while he was in such an ignominious position I had little desire for his society. And as he was perpetually in a kind of somnambulistic state, I quitted Trouville without having exchanged a dozen words with my unhappy friend, whom I left a prey to the Cères and Countess V——.

One evening in Paris I met him again. It was at the house of his friends and neighbours, the N——'s, who are charming hosts. In the arrangement of their beautiful house in the Avenue Kléber, I recognized the excellent taste of Madame N—— united to that of Du Fau, and blending very harmoniously together. There were not many present, only a few friends. As in the past, Paul Du Fau displayed that turn of wit peculiar to him, that refined delicacy touched with a flavour of the most picturesque brutality. Madame N—— is intelligent and the conversation in her salon is quite good. Nevertheless when I first entered the talk was extremely commonplace. A magistrate, Monsieur le Conseiller Nicolas, was relating at length that hackneyed tale of the sentry box, wherein every sentinel in turn committed suicide, and which had to be pulled down in order to put a stop to this novel epidemic. After which Madame N—— asked me if I believed in talismans. Monsieur le Conseiller Nicolas relieved my embarrassment by saying that I, being an unbeliever, was bound to be superstitious.

" You are quite right," replied Madame N——. " He believes neither in God nor the devil. And he adores stories of the other world."

I looked at this charming woman while she was speaking ; and I admired the unobtrusive grace of her cheeks, her neck and her shoulders. Her whole person gives one the idea of something rare and precious. I do not know what Du Fau thinks of Madame N——'s foot. To me it is beautiful.

Paul Du Fau came and shook hands with me. I noticed that he was no longer wearing his ring.

" What have you done with your amethyst ? "

" I have lost it."

" What ! An intaglio more beautiful than any in Rome and Naples ! You have lost it ? "

Without giving him time to reply, N——, who is always at his side, exclaimed :

" Yes, it is a curious story. He has lost his amethyst."

N—— is an excellent fellow, very self confident,

a trifle diffuse, and of a simplicity which sometimes provokes a smile.   Noisily he called to his wife :

" Marthe, my love, here is some one who has not yet heard that Du Fau has lost his amethyst."

And turning to me :

" Why, it is quite a story.   Would you believe it ? Our friend had absolutely forsaken us.   I used to say to my wife: ' What have you done to Du Fau ? ' She would reply: ' What have I done ? Why nothing, my love.'   It was incomprehensible.   But our astonishment doubled when we heard that he was always with that poor Madame Cère."

Madame N——— interrupted her husband :

" What has that got to do with it ? "

But N——— insisted :

" Excuse me, my love !   But I must mention it in order to explain the history of the amethyst.   Well, this summer our friend Du Fau refused to come with us to the country as he had been in the habit of doing. My wife and I had given him a very hearty invitation.   But he remained at Trouville, with his cousin de Maureil, in very dull society."

Madame N——— protested.

" It is true," repeated N———, " very dull society. He spent his time going out in a boat with Madame Cère."

Du Fau calmly observed that there was not one word of truth in what N—— was saying. The latter putting his hand on his friend's shoulder said:

" I defy you to contradict me."

And he finished his story.

" Day and night Du Fau went out with Madame Cère, or with her ghost, for it is said that Madame Cère is nothing but the ghost of her former self. Cère stayed on the beach with his field-glasses. During one of these excursions Du Fau lost his amethyst. After this mischance he declined to stay a day longer at Trouville. He left the place without bidding anyone farewell, took train and came to us, at Les Eyzies, where we had given up expecting him. It was two o'clock in the morning. 'Here I am,' he said calmly. There's eccentricity for you ! "

" And the amethyst ? " I asked.

" It is true," replied Du Fau, " that it fell into the sea. It lies buried in the sand. At least no fisherman has in the traditional manner brought it to land in the belly of a fish."

A few days later, I paid one of my customary visits to Hendel in the Rue de Chateaudun. And I inquired whether he had not some curiosity with which to tempt me. He knows that I am so old fashioned

L

as to collect ancient bronzes and marbles. Silently
he opened a glass case, reserved for amateurs, and
took out a little Egyptian scribe in pietra dura,
of primitive workmanship, a veritable treasure!
When I heard its price, I myself put it back, not
without a longing glance. Then in the case I perceived the imprint in wax of the intaglio I had so
much admired at Du Fau's. I recognized the
nymph, the pillar, the laurel. It was beyond the
possibility of a doubt.

" Did you ever have the gem ? " I asked Hendel.

" Yes, I sold it last year."

" A fine gem ! Where did you get it ? "

" It came from the collection of Mark Delion,
the financier, who five years ago committed suicide
on account of a society lady. . . . Madame . . .
perhaps you know her . . . Madame Cère.

LA SIGNORA CHIARA

TO UGO OJETTI

LA SIGNORA CHIARA

ROFESSOR GIACOMO TEDESCHI of Naples is a doctor well known in the town. His house, which is decidedly odoriferous, is near the Incoronata. It is frequented by all kinds of persons, and particularly by the beautiful maidens who at Santa Lucia traffic in the harvest of the sea. He sells drugs for all maladies ; he is not above extracting a decayed tooth ; he is an adept, the day after a festival, at sewing up the gaping skin of a bravo ; and he knows how to use the long shore dialect interspersed with academical Latin so as to impart confidence to his patients laid out on the longest, the most rickety, the most creaking and the dirtiest operating-chair to be found in any seaport in the universe. He is a man of slender build, of full face, with little green eyes and a long nose overhanging a thin-lipped mouth ; his round shoulders, his pot belly and his thin legs recall the pantaloon of bygone times.

Late in life Giacomo married the young Chiara Mammi, daughter of an old convict highly esteemed in Naples, who, having become a baker on the Borgo di Santo, died lamented by the whole town. Ripened by the sun which gilds the grapes of Torre and the oranges of Sorrento, the beauty of Chiara blossomed in glowing splendour.

Professor Giacomo Tedeschi held the fitting belief that his wife was as virtuous as she was beautiful. Moreover he knew how strong is the sentiment of feminine honour in a bandit's family. But he was a doctor and aware of the disturbances and weaknesses to which the nature of woman is liable. He felt some anxiety when Ascanio Ranieri of Milan, who had set up as ladies' tailor on the Piazza dei Martiri, took to visiting his house. Ascanio was young, handsome and always smiling. The daughter of the heroic Mammi, the patriot baker, was certainly too good a Neapolitan to forget her duty with a townsman of Milan. Nevertheless Ascanio showed a preference for visiting the house near the Incoronata during the doctor's absence, and the signora willingly received him unchaperoned.

One day when the Professor came home earlier than he was expected, he surprised Ascanio on his knees to Chiara. While the signora departed with the measured step of a goddess, Ascanio rose to his feet.

Giacomo Tedeschi approached him with every sign of the most anxious solicitude.

" My friend, I see that you are ill. You did well to come to see me. I am a doctor and vowed to the relief of human suffering. You are in pain, do not deny it. Your face is aflame. It is headache, an acute headache, doubtless. How wise of you to come to see me. You were waiting for me impatiently, I am sure. Yes, a terrible headache. While uttering these words, the old man, strong as a Sabine bull, was pushing Ascanio into his consulting-room and forcing him to recline in that famous operating-chair, which for forty years had borne the weight of suffering Neapolitans.

Then holding him inexorably there:

" I see what it is, your tooth is aching. That's it ! Yes, your toothache is very bad."

He took from a case an enormous dentist's forceps, prised open his capacious mouth and with a turn of the forceps pulled out a tooth.

Ascanio fled, spitting blood from his streaming jaw, and Professor Giacomo Tedeschi shrieked after him with savage joy:

" A fine tooth ! a fine, a very fine tooth ! . . ."

UPRIGHT JUDGES

TO MADAME MARCELLE TINAYRE

UPRIGHT JUDGES

"UPRIGHT judges I have indeed seen," said Jean Marteau. "It was in a picture. I had gone to Belgium to escape from an inquisitive magistrate, who insisted that I had conspired with anarchists. I did not know my accomplices and my accomplices did not know me. But that presented no difficulty to the magistrate. Nothing embarrassed him. Though he was perpetually weighing evidence his sense of values remained undeveloped. His persistence terrified me. I went to Belgium and stopped at Antwerp, where I became a grocer's assistant. In the picture gallery one Sunday I saw two upright judges in a painting by Mabuse. They are of a type now extinct. I mean the type of peripatetic judges who used to travel at a jog-trot on their ambling nags. Foot soldiers, armed with lances and partisans form their escort. Bearded and hairy, these two judges, like the kings in old Flemish bibles, wear an eccentric yet magnificent headdress suggestive at once of a nightcap and a diadem. Their brocaded robes are richly adorned. The old master has succeeded in imparting to them a grave, calm and gentle air. Their horses are as mild and calm as they. Nevertheless these two judges differed both in character and in point of view. You can see that at once. One holds a paper in his hand and with his finger points to the text. The other, his left hand on the pommel of his saddle, is raising his right with more benevolence than authority. Between thumb and forefinger he appears to be holding an impalpable powder. And the hand thus carefully posed for this gesture suggests an intellect cautious and subtle. They are upright both of them, but obviously the first adheres to the letter, the second to the spirit. Leaning against the rail which separates them from the public, I listened to their talk. Said the first judge:

" I hold to the written word. The first law was written on stone as a sign that it would last as long as the world."

The other judge made answer:

" Every law is out of date as soon as it is written. For the hand of the scribe is slow, the mind of man is nimble and his destiny is uncertain."

Then these two excellent old men pursued their sententious discussion :

First judge. The law is stable.

Second judge. The law is never fixed.

First judge. Coming forth frcm God it is immutable.

Second judge. Proceeding naturally from society it is dependent upon the changing conditions of this life.

First judge. It is the will of God, which changeth not.

Second judge. It is the will of man which changeth ever.

First judge. It was before man and is superior to him.

Second judge. It is of man, infirm as he, and like unto him capable of perfection.

First judge. Judge, open thy book and read what is written therein. For it is God who dictated to such as believed in Him : *Sic locutus est patribus nostris, Abraham et semini ejus in sæcula.*

Second judge. That which is written by the dead will be erased by the living. Were it not so, the will of those who have passed away would impose itself upon those who yet survive ; and the dead would be the living and the living the dead.

First judge. To laws prescribed by the dead the living owe obedience. The quick and the dead are contemporary before God. Moses and Cyrus, Cæsar, Justinian and the Emperor of Almaine yet reign over us. For in the sight of the Eternal One we are their contemporaries.

Second judge. The living owe obedience to the laws prescribed by the living. For our instruction in that which is permitted and that which is forbidden Zoroaster and Numa Pompilius rank below the cobbler of Saint Gudule.

First judge. The first laws were revealed to us by the Infinite Wisdom. The best laws are those which are nearest to that source.

Second judge. Do you not see that every day new laws are made and that Constitutions and codes differ according to time and place ?

First judge. New laws proceed from those that are ancient. They are the young branches of the same tree nourished by the same sap.

Second judge. From the ancient tree of the law there is distilled a bitter juice. Ceaselessly is the axe laid unto that tree.

First judge. It is not for the judge to inquire whether the laws are just, since they must necessarily be so. He has only to administer them justly.

Second judge. It is for us to inquire whether the law that we administer be just or unjust, because if we discover it to be unjust, it is possible for us to introduce some modification into the application we are forced to make of it.

First judge. The criticism of laws is not compatible with the respect we owe to them.

Second judge. If we do not recognize the severity of the law how can we temper it ?

First judge. We are judges, not legislators or philosophers.

Second judge. We are men.

First judge. A man is incapable of judging men. A judge, when he goes to the seat of justice, puts off his humanity. He assumes divinity and no longer tastes either joy or sorrow.

Second judge. When justice is not dispensed with sympathy it becomes the cruellest injustice.

First judge. Justice is perfect when it is literal.

Second judge. When justice is not spiritual it is absurd.

First judge. The principle of laws is divine and the consequences which flow from them are no less divine. But even if law were not wholly of God, if it were wholly of man, it would still be necessary to administer it according to the letter. For the letter is fixed, the spirit is fleeting.

Second judge. Law is wholly of man. It was born foolish and cruel in the early glimmerings of human reason. But were it of divine essence, it should be followed according to the spirit not according to the letter, for the letter is dead and the spirit is living.

Having thus conversed, the two upright judges dismounted and with their escort approached the Tribunal, whither they must go, in order to render unto each man his due. Their horses, tied to a stake, under a great elm, conversed together. The first judge's horse spoke first :

" When horses inherit the earth," he said (and the earth will doubtless belong to them one day, for the horse is obviously the ultimate end and the final object of creation), "when the earth is the horse's and we are free to act as we will, we will live under laws like men and we will take delight in imprisoning, hanging and breaking on the wheel our fellow creatures. We will be moral beings. It shall be proved by the prisons, the gibbets and the strappados which shall be erected in our towns. There shall be legislative horses. What do you think Roussin ? "

Roussin, who was the second judge's steed, replied

that in his opinion the horse was the king of creation and he confidently hoped that sooner or later his kingdom would come.

" And when we have built towns, Blanchet," he added, " we must, as you say, establish a system of police in them. In those days I would have the laws of horses equine, that is favourable to horses and for the equine weal."

" What do you mean by that, Roussin ? " asked Blanchet.

" My meaning is the natural one. I demand that the law shall secure for each his share of corn and his place in the stable, and that each be permitted to love as he will during the season. For there is a time for everything. In short I would have the laws of horses in conformity with nature."

" I hope," replied Blanchet, " that the ideas of our legislators will be more elevated than yours, Blanchet. They will make laws according as they are inspired by that celestial horse who has created all horses. He is all good since he is all powerful. Power and goodness are his attributes. He foreordained his creatures to endure the bit, to drag at the halter, to feel the spur and to die beneath the whip. You talk of love, comrade ; he ordained that many of us should be made geldings. It is his

M

command.   The laws must maintain this worshipful behest.

"But are you quite sure, my friend," inquired Roussin, "that these evils proceed from the celestial horse that has created us, and not merely from man his inferior creation ?"

"Men are the ministers and the angels of the celestial horse," replied Blanchet. "His will is manifest in everything that happens. His will is good. Since he wishes us ill, it must be that ill is good. If therefore the law is to do us good it must make us suffer. And in the Empire of horses we shall be constrained and tortured in every way, by means of edicts, decrees, sentences, judgments and ordinances in order to please the heavenly horse."

"Roussin," added Blanchet, "you must have the head of an ass not to understand that the horse was brought into the world to suffer, and that if he does not suffer he fails to fulfil his destiny and that from happy horses the heavenly horse turns away his face."

THE OCEAN CHRIST

TO IVAN STRANNIK

THE OCEAN CHRIST

HAT year many of the fishers of Saint-Valéry had been drowned at sea. Their bodies were found on the beach cast up by the waves with the wreckage of their boats ; and for nine days, up the steep road leading to the church were to be seen coffins borne by hand and followed by widows, who were weeping beneath their great black-hooded cloaks, like women in the Bible.

Thus were the skipper Jean Lenoël and his son Désiré laid in the great nave, beneath the vaulted roof from which they had once hung a ship in full rigging as an offering to Our Lady. They were righteous men and God-fearing. Monsieur Guillaume Truphème, priest of Saint-Valéry, having pronounced the Absolution, said in a tearful voice :

"Never were laid in consecrated ground there to await the judgment of God better men and better Christians than Jean Lenoël and his son Désiré."

And while barques and their skippers perished near the coast, in the high seas great vessels foundered. Not a day passed that the ocean did not bring in some flotsam of wreck. Now one morning some children who were steering a boat saw a figure lying on the sea. It was a figure of Jesus Christ, life-size, carved in wood, painted in natural colouring, and looking as if it were very old. The Good Lord was floating upon the sea with arms outstretched. The children towed the figure ashore and brought it up into Saint-Valéry. The head was encircled with the crown of thorns. The feet and hands were pierced. But the nails were missing as well as the cross. The arms were still outstretched ready for sacrifice and blessing, just as He appeared to Joseph of Arimathea and the holy women when they were burying him.

The children gave it to Monsieur le Curé Truphème, who said to them :

" This image of the Saviour is of ancient workmanship. He who made it must have died long ago. Although to-day in the shops of Amiens and Paris excellent statues are sold for a hundred francs and more, we must admit that the earlier sculptors were not without merit. But what delights me most is the thought that if Jesus Christ be thus come with

open arms to Saint-Valéry, it is in order to bless the
parish, which has been so cruelly tried, and in order
to announce that he has compassion on the poor
folk who go a-fishing at the risk of their lives.   He
is the God who walked upon the sea and blessed the
nets of Cephas."

And Monsieur le Curé Truphème, having had
the Christ placed in the church on the cloth of the
high altar, went off to order from the carpenter
Lemerre a beautiful cross in heart of oak.

When it was made, the Saviour was nailed to it
with brand new nails, and it was erected in the nave
above the churchwarden's pew.

Then it was noticed that His eyes were filled with
mercy and seemed to glisten with tears of heavenly
pity.

One of the churchwardens, who was present at
the putting up of the crucifix, fancied he saw tears
streaming down the divine face.   The next morning
when Monsieur le Curé with a choir-boy entered the
church to say his mass, he was astonished to find the
cross above the churchwarden's pew empty and the
Christ lying upon the altar.

As soon as he had celebrated the divine sacrifice
he had the carpenter called and asked him why he
had taken the Christ down from his cross.   But the

carpenter replied that he had not touched it. Then, after having questioned the beadle and the sidesmen, Monsieur Truphème made certain that no one had entered the church since the crucifix had been placed over the churchwarden's pew.

Thereupon he felt that these things were miraculous, and he meditated upon them discreetly. The following Sunday in his exhortation he spoke of them to his parishioners, and he called upon them to contribute by their gifts to the erection of a new cross more beautiful than the first and more worthy to bear the Redeemer of the world.

The poor fishers of Saint-Valéry gave as much money as they could and the widows brought their wedding-rings. Wherefore Monsieur Truphème was able to go at once to Abbeville and to order a cross of ebony, highly polished and surmounted by a scroll with the inscription I.N.R.I. in letters of gold. Two months later it was erected in the place of the former and the Christ was nailed to it between the lance and the sponge.

But Jesus left this cross as He had left the other ; and as soon as night fell He went and stretched Himself upon the altar.

Monsieur le Curé, when he found Him there in the morning, fell on his knees and prayed for a long while.

The fame of this miracle spread throughout the
neighbourhood, and the ladies of Amiens made a
collection for the Christ of Saint-Valéry.   Monsieur
Truphème received money and jewels from Paris,
and the wife of the Minister of Marine, Madame
Hyde de Neuville, sent him a heart of diamonds.
Of all these treasures, in the space of two years, a
goldsmith of La Rue St. Sulpice, fashioned a cross
of gold and precious stones which was set up
with great pomp in the church of Saint-Valéry on
the second Sunday after Easter in the year 18—.
But He who had not refused the cross of sorrow,
fled from this cross of gold and again stretched Himself upon the white linen of the altar.

For fear of offending Him, He was left there
this time ; and He had lain upon the altar for
more than two years, when Pierre, son of Pierre
Caillou, came to tell Monsieur le Curé Truphème
that he had found the true cross of Our Lord on
the beach.

Pierre was an innocent ; and, because he had not
sense enough to earn a livelihood, people gave him
bread out of charity, he was liked because he never
did any harm.   But he wandered in his talk and no
one listened to him.

Nevertheless Monsieur Truphème, who had never

ceased meditating on the Ocean Christ, was struck by what the poor imbecile had just said. With the beadle and two sidesmen he went to the spot, where the child said he had seen a cross, and there he found two planks studded with nails, which had long been washed by the sea and which did indeed form a cross.

They were the remains of some old shipwreck. On one of these boards could still be read two letters painted in black, a J and an L ; and there was no doubt that this was a fragment of Jean Lenoël's barque, he who with his son Désiré had been lost at sea five years before.

At the sight of this, the beadle and the sidesmen began to laugh at the innocent who had taken the broken planks of a boat for the cross of Jesus Christ. But Monsieur le Curé Truphème checked their merriment. He had meditated much and prayed long since the Ocean Christ had arrived among the fisherfolk, and the mystery of infinite charity began to dawn upon him. He knelt down upon the sand, repeated the prayer for the faithful departed, and then told the beadle and the sidesmen to carry the flotsam on their shoulders and to place it in the church. When this had been done he raised the Christ from the altar, placed it on the planks of the boat and himself nailed it to them, with the nails that the ocean had corroded.

By the priest's command, the very next day this cross took the place of the cross of gold and precious stones over the churchwarden's pew. The Ocean Christ has never left it. He has chosen to remain nailed to the planks on which men died invoking His name and that of His Mother. There, with parted lips, august and afflicted He seems to say:

" My cross is made of all men's woes, for I am in truth the God of the poor and the heavy-laden."

JEAN MARTEAU

JEAN MARTEAU

I

A DREAM

THE talk fell on sleep and dreams.

Jean Marteau said that one dream had left an indelible impression on his mind.

"Was it a prophetic dream?" inquired Monsieur Goubin.

"In itself," replied Jean Marteau, "the dream was not remarkable, not even for its incoherence. But its images presented themselves with a painful vividness which is quite unique. Nothing I ever experienced, nothing, was ever so real to me, so actual as the visions of this dream. In that lies its interest. It enabled me to understand the illusions of a mystic. Had I been less rational I should certainly have taken it to be an apocalypse and a revelation, and I should have derived therefrom principles of conduct and a rule of life. I ought to tell you that I dreamed this dream under peculiar circumstances. It was in the spring of 1895; I was twenty. Having recently arrived in Paris I was in difficulties. That night I had lain down in a copse of the Versailles wood. I had eaten nothing for twenty-four hours. I suffered no pain. I was in a state of calm and ease, disturbed occasionally by a feeling of anxiety. It seemed to me as if I was neither asleep nor awake. A little girl, quite a little girl in a blue-hooded cape, and a white apron, was walking with crutches over a plain. With every step she took her crutches grew and raised her like stilts. They soon became higher than the poplars on the river's bank. A woman who *saw* my surprise said to me: "Don't you know that in the spring crutches grow ? But there are times when the size increases with alarming rapidity."

A man whose face I could not see, added : " It is the climacteric hour."

Then with a soft and mysterious sound which alarmed me, all around me the grass began to grow. I arose and reached a plain covered with wan plants, cottony and dead. There I met Vernaux, who was my only friend in Paris, where he lived as penuriously as I. Long we walked side by side in silence. In the sky the stars, huge and rayless, were like discs of pale gold.

I knew the cause of this appearance and I explained it to Vernaux: " It is an optical phenomenon," I said, " our eyes are out of focus."

And with infinite care and minuteness I engaged in a demonstration which chiefly turned upon the exact correspondence between the human eye and the astronomical telescope. While I was reasoning thus, Vernaux found on the ground some leaden-coloured grass, an enormous black hat, boat shaped, with a brim, a band of gold braid and a diamond buckle. Putting it on his head, he said: " It is the lord mayor's hat." " Obviously," I replied, and I resumed my demonstration. So arduous was it that the perspiration dropped from my forehead. I was always losing the thread and beginning again vaguely with the phrase: " The great saurians who swam in the tepid waters of the primitive ocean had eyes constructed like a telescope. . . ."

I continued until I perceived that Vernaux had disappeared. It was not long before I found him again in a hollow. He was on a spit, roasting over a brushwood fire. Indians with their hair tied on the tops of their heads were basting him with a long-handled spoon and were turning the spit. In a clear voice Vernaux said to me : "Mélanie has been here."

Then only did I perceive that he had the head and neck of a chicken.   But all I could think of was how to find Mélanie, who, by a sudden inspiration I knew to be the most beautiful of women.   I ran, and, having reached the edge of a wood, by the moonlight I saw a white form fleeting before me.   Hair of a glorious red fell over her neck.   A silver light caressed her shoulders, a blue shadow filled the hollow in the middle of her gleaming back; and, as she ran, her dimples in their rise and fall seemed to smile with a divine smile.   I distinctly saw the azure shadow on her leg augment or diminish according to the motion of the limb.   I noticed also the pink soles of her feet.   Long did I pursue her without fatigue and with a step light as the flight of a bird. But a dark shadow veiled her, and her perpetual flight led me into a path so narrow that it was blocked completely by a little iron stove.   It was one of those stoves with long bent pipes which are used in studios.   It was at a white heat.   The door was incandescent and all around the metal was red hot. A cat with its hair all shorn was sitting on it and looking at me.   As I drew near I perceived through the cracks in its scorched skin an ardent mass of liquid

metal which filled its body.   It was miauling, and I
understood that it was asking for water.   In order
to find some, I descended the slope on which was
a cool wood of birch and ash trees.   A stream ran
through it at the bottom of a ravine.   But I could
not approach it on account of the blocks of sandstone
and tufts of dwarf oaks by which it was overhung.
As I slipped on a mossy stone my left arm came away
from my shoulder without causing a wound or any
pain.   I took it in my right hand ; it was cold and
numb ; its touch made me shudder.   I reflected
that now I was in danger of losing it and how weari-
some a drudgery it would be for the rest of my life
to have to watch ceaselessly over it.   I resolved to
order an ebony box wherein I might keep it when it
was not in use.   As it was very cold in this damp
hollow I quitted it by a rustic path which led me on
to a wind-swept plateau, where all the trees were
bent as if in sorrow.   There along a yellow road
a procession was passing.   It was countrified and
humble, just like the Rogation procession in the
village of Brécé, which our Master, Monsieur
Bergeret, knows so well.   There was nothing singular
about the clergy, the confraternities, or the faithful
except that no one had any feet and that they all
moved upon little wheels.   Under the canopy I

recognized Monsieur l'Abbé Lantaigne, who had become village priest and was weeping tears of blood. I wanted to call out to him : " I am *ministre pleni-potentiaire.*" But my voice choked in my throat, and a great shadow coming down upon me caused me to raise my head. It was one of the little lame girl's crutches. They had now ascended into the sky some thousand metres, and I perceived the child like a little black spot against the moon. The stars had grown still larger and paler, and among them I distinguished three planets, the spherical form of which was quite visible to the eye. I even thought I could recognize spots on their surface. But these spots did not correspond to the drawings of those on Mars, Jupiter and Saturn which I had once seen in astronomical books.

My friend Vernaux having come up, I asked him whether he could not see the canals on the planet Mars. " The Ministry is defeated," he said.

He bore no sign of the spit I had seen transfixing him, but he still had a chicken's head and neck, and he was dripping with gravy. I felt an uncontrollable desire to demonstrate my optical theory to him and to resume my argument where I had left it. " The great saurians," I said, " which swam in the tepid waters of the primitive ocean had eyes constructed like a telescope. . . ."

Instead of listening to me, he went up to a reading-desk, which was there in the field, opened an antiphonary and began to crow like a cock.

Out of all patience, I turned my back on him and jumped into a tram that was passing. Inside I found a vast dining-hall, like those in great hotels or on board Atlantic liners. It was all flowers and glass. As far as one could see there were seated at table women in low frocks and men in evening dress in front of candelabra and crystal chandeliers forming an infinite vista of light. A steward came round with meat to which I helped myself. But it emitted a disgusting odour and it made me feel sick before I tasted it. Besides *I was not hungry.* The diners left the table before I had swallowed a mouthful. While the servants were taking away the candles Vernaux came up to me and said: " You did not notice the lady in the low-necked dress who was sitting next you. It was Mélanie. Look."

And through the door he pointed to shoulders flooded with a white light, out in the darkness under the trees. I leapt out, I rushed in pursuit of the charming form. This time I caught it up, I touched it. For one moment I felt a delicious throbbing beneath my fingers. But she slipped from my arms and I was embracing briars.

That was my dream.

" Truly your dream was sad," said Monsieur Bergeret, to quote the simple Stratonice :

" ' A vision of oneself may arouse no little disgust.' "

THE LAW IS DEAD BUT THE JUDGE
IS LIVING

FEW days later, said Jean Marteau, I happened to be lying in a thicket of the Bois de Vincennes. I had eaten nothing for thirty-six hours.

Monsieur Goubin wiped his eye-glasses. His eyes were kind but his glance was keen. He looked hard at Jean Marteau and said to him reproachfully:

"What? Again you had eaten nothing for twenty-four hours?"

"Again," replied Jean Marteau, "I had eaten nothing for twenty-four hours. But I was wrong. One ought not to go without food. It is not right. Hunger should be a crime like vagrancy. But as a matter of fact the two offences are regarded as one and the same; article 269 inflicts from three to six months' imprisonment on those who lack

means of subsistence. Vagrancy, according to the
code, is the condition of vagrants, of vagabonds,
persons without any fixed dwelling or means of
subsistence, who exercise no specific trade or profession. They are great criminals."

" It is curious," said Monsieur Bergeret, " that the
state of vagrancy, punishable by six months' imprisonment and ten years' police supervision, is precisely
the same as that in which the good St. Francis
placed his companions at St. Mary of the Angels
and the daughters of St. Clare. If St. Francis of
Assisi and St. Anthony of Padua came to preach in
Paris to-day they would run great risk of being
clapped into the prison van and carried off to the
police court. Not that I mean to denounce to
the authorities the mendicant monks who now
swarm among us. They possess means of livelihood ;
they exercise all manner of trades."

" They are respectable because they are rich,"
said Jean Marteau. " It is only the poor who are
forbidden to beg. Had I been discovered beneath
my tree I should have been thrown into prison and
that would have been justice. Possessing nothing,
I was assumed to be the enemy of property ; and
it is just to defend property against its enemies.
The august task of the judge is to assure to every

man that which belongs to him, to the rich his wealth, to the poor his poverty."

" I have reflected on the philosophy of law," said Monsieur Bergeret, " and I have perceived that the whole structure of social justice rests upon two axioms : robbery is to be condemned : the result of robbery is to be respected. These are the principles which assure the security of individuals and maintain order in the State. If one of these tutelary principles were to be disregarded the whole of society would fall to pieces. They were established in the beginning of time. A chief clothed in bearskin, armed with an axe of flint and with a sword of bronze, returned with his comrades to the stone entrenchments, wherein were enclosed the children of the tribe and the troops of women and of reindeer. They brought back with them youths and maidens from the neighbouring tribe and stones fallen from the sky, which were precious because out of them could be made swords which would not bend. The chief ascended a hillock in the middle of the enclosure and said: ' These slaves and this iron, which I have taken from men weak and contemptible are mine. Whosoever shall lay hands upon them shall be struck down by my axe.' Such is the origin of law. Its spirit is ancient and barbarous. And it is

because justice is the ratification of all injustice that
it reassures every one.

"A judge may be benevolent, for men are not all
bad ; the law cannot be benevolent because it is
anterior to all ideas of benevolence. The changes
which have been introduced into it down the ages
have not altered its original character. Jurists have
rendered it subtle, but they have left it barbaric.
Its very ferocity causes it to be respected and regarded as august. Men are given to worship malevolent gods, and that which is not cruel seems to them
not worth their adoration. The judged believe in
the justice of laws. Their morality is that of the
judges ; both one and the other. believe that a
punished action is penal. In the police court or at
the assizes I have often been touched to see how
the accused and the judge agree perfectly in their
ideas of good and evil. They have the same prejudices and a common morality."

"It cannot be otherwise," said Jean Marteau.
"A poor creature who has stolen from a shop
window a sausage or a pair of shoes has not
on that account looked deeply and boldly into
the very origin of law and the foundation of
justice. And those who like ourselves are not
afraid to behold in the origin of Codes a sanction

of violence and iniquity, are incapable of stealing a halfpenny."

" But after all," said Monsieur Goubin, "there are just laws."

" Do you think so ? " inquired Jean Marteau.

" Monsieur Goubin is right," said Monsieur Bergeret. " There are just laws. But law having been instituted for the defence of society, in its spirit cannot be more equitable than that society. As long as society is founded upon injustice the function of laws will be to defend and maintain that injustice. And the more unjust they are the worthier of respect they will appear. Notice also that, ancient as most of them are, they do not exactly represent present unrighteousness but past unrighteousnesses which is ruder and crasser. They are monuments of the Dark Ages which have lingered on into brighter days."

" But they are being improved," said Monsieur Goubin.

" They are being improved," said Monsieur Bergeret. " The Chamber and the Senate work at them when they have nothing else to do. But the heart of them remains ; and it is bitter. To be frank, I should not greatly fear bad laws if they were administered by good judges. The law is unbending, it is said, I do not believe it. There is no text which may not receive various interpretations. The law is dead. The magistrate is living: he possesses this great advantage over the law. Unfortunately he seldom uses it. Generally he schools himself to be colder, more insensible, more dead than the code he applies. He is not human ; he knows no pity. In him the caste spirit stifles all human sympathy.

" I am only speaking now of honest judges."

"They are in the majority," said Monsieur Goubin.

" They are in the majority," replied Monsieur Bergeret, " if we refer to common honesty and every-day morals. But is an approach to common honesty sufficient equipment for a man who, without falling into error or abuse has to wield the enormous power of punishing ? A good judge should possess at once a kind heart and a philosophic mind. That is much to ask from a man who has his way to make and is determined to win advancement in his profession. Leaving out of account the fact that if he displays a morality superior to that of his day he will be hated by his fellows and will arouse universal indignation. For we condemn as immoral all morality which is not our own. All who have introduced any novel goodness into the world have met with the scorn of honest folk. That is what happened to President Magnaud.

" I have his judgments here, collected in a little volume with commentaries by Henri Leyret. When these judgments were pronounced they provoked the indignation of austere magistrates and virtuous legislators. They are stamped with noble thoughts and tender kindness. They are full of pity, they are human, they are virtuous. In the Law Courts President Magnaud was thought not to have a judicial mind, and the friends of Monsieur Méline accused him of lacking respect for property. And it is true that the considerations on which the judgments of President Magnaud repose are singular, for at every line one meets the thoughts of an independent mind and the sentiments of a generous heart."

Taking from the table a little crimson volume, Monsieur Bergeret turned over the pages and read :

" *Honesty and delicacy are two virtues infinitely easier to practise when one lacks nothing than when one is destitute of everything.*"

" *That which cannot be avoided ought not to be punished.*"

" *In order to judge equitably the crime of the poor the judge should for the moment forget his own well-*

being, in order as far as possible to place himself in the sad situation of a being whom every one has deserted."

" In his interpretation of the law the judge should not merely bear in mind the special case which is submitted to him, he should take into consideration the wider consequences for good or for evil which his sentence may involve."

" It is the workman alone who produces and who risks his health or his life for the exclusive profit of his master, who endangers nothing but his capital."

" I have quoted almost haphazard," added Monsieur Bergeret, closing the book. " These are novel words. They are the echo of a great soul."

MONSIEUR THOMAS

MONSIEUR THOMAS

I ONCE knew an austere judge. His name was Thomas de Maulan. He was a country gentleman. During the seven years ministry of Marshal MacMahon he had become a magistrate in the hope that one day he would administer justice in the king's name. He had principles which he believed to be unalterable, having never attempted to examine them. As soon as one examines a principle one discovers something beneath it and perceives that it was not a principle at all. Both his religious and his social principles Thomas de Maulan kept outside the range of his curiosity.

He was judge in the court of first instance in the little town of X——, where I was then living. His appearance inspired esteem and even a certain sympathy. His figure was tall, thin, and bony, his face was sallow. His extreme simplicity gave him a somewhat distinguished air. He liked to be called Monsieur Thomas, not that he despised his social position, but because he considered himself too poor to support it. I knew enough of him to recognize that his appearance was not deceptive and that though weak in character and narrow in intelligence he had a noble soul. I discovered that he possessed high moral qualities. But, having had occasion to observe him in the fulfilment of his functions as examining magistrate and judge, I perceived that his very uprightness and his conception of duty rendered him cruel and sometimes completely deprived him of insight. His extreme piety caused him to be unconsciously obsessed by the ideas of sin and expiation, of crime and punishment; and it was obvious that in punishing criminals he experienced the agreeable sensation of purifying them. Human justice he regarded as a faint yet beautiful reflection of divine justice. In childhood he had been taught that suffering is good, that it is a merit in itself, a virtue, an expiation. This he believed firmly; and he held that suffering is the due of whomsoever has sinned. He loved to chastise. His punishments were the outcome of his kindness of his heart. Accustomed to give thanks to the God who, for his eternal salvation, afflicted

him with toothache and colic as a punishment
for Adam's sin, he sentenced vagrants and vagabonds to imprisonment and reparation as one who
bestows benefits.   His legal philosophy was founded
upon his catechism ; his pitilessness proceeded from
his directness and simplicity of mind.   One could
not call him cruel.   But not being sensual neither
was he sensitive.   He had no precise physical idea
of human suffering.   His conception of it was purely
moral and dogmatic.   There was something mystic
in his preference for the system of solitary confine-
ment, and it was not without a certain joyfulness
of heart and eye that one day he showed me over
a fine prison which had recently been built in
his district : a white thing, clean, silent, terrible ;
cells arranged in a circle, and the warder in the
centre in an observation chamber.   It looked like
a laboratory constructed by lunatics for the manu-
facture of lunatics.   And malevolent lunatics indeed
are those inventors of the solitary system who in
order to convert a wrongdoer into a moral being
subject him to a régime which turns him into an
imbecile or a savage.   That was not the opinion of
Monsieur Thomas.   He gazed with silent satisfaction on those atrocious cells.   At the back of his
mind was the idea that the prisoner is never alone

since God is with him.   And his calm, self-satisfied glance seemed to say: " Here I have brought five or six persons face to face with their Creator and Sovereign Judge.   There is no more enviable fate in the world."

It fell to this magistrate's lot to conduct the inquiry in several cases, among others in that of a teacher. Lay and clerical education were then at open war. The republicans having denounced the ignorance and brutality of the priests, the clerical newspaper of the district accused a lay teacher of having made a child sit on a red-hot stove.   Among the country aristocracy this accusation found credence.   Revolting details were related and the common gossip aroused the attention of justice.   Monsieur Thomas, who was an honest man, would never have listened to his passions, had he known them to be passions. But he regarded them as duties because they were religious.   He believed it to be his duty to consider complaints urged against a godless school, and he failed to perceive his extreme eagerness to consider them.   I must not omit to say that he conducted the inquiry with meticulous care and infinite trouble.   He conducted it according to the ordinary methods of justice, and he obtained wonderful results.   Thirty school children, persistently interrogated, replied at first badly, afterwards better, and finally very well. After a month's examination, they replied so well that they all gave the same answer. The thirty depositions agreed, they were identical, literally identical, and these children who on the first day said they had seen nothing, now declared with one unfaltering voice, employing exactly the same words, that their little schoolfellow had been seated bare-skinned, on a red-hot stove. Monsieur le Juge Thomas was congratulating himself on so satisfactory a result, when the teacher proved irrefutably that there had never been a stove in the school. Then Monsieur Thomas began to suspect that the children were lying. But what he never perceived was that he himself had unwittingly dictated their evidence and taught it to them by heart.

The prosecution was nonsuited. The teacher was dismissed the court after having been severely reprimanded by the judge, who strongly urged him in the future to restrain his brutal instincts. Outside his deserted school the priest's scholars made a hullaballoo. And when he went out he was greeted with cries of " Ha ! ha ! *Grille-Cul* (Roast-back) " ; and stones were thrown at him. The Inspector of Primary Schools being informed of the state of affairs, drew up a report stating that this teacher had no authority over his pupils and concluding that his immediate transference to another school would be advisable. He was sent to a village where a dialect was spoken which he did not understand. Even there he was called *Grille-Cul*. It was the only French term that was known there.

During my intercourse with Monsieur Thomas I learnt how all evidence given before an examining magistrate comes to be uniform in style. He received me in his room whilst with the assistance of his clerk he was examining a witness. I was about to withdraw, but he begged me to remain, saying that my presence would in no way interfere with a proper administration of justice.

I sat down in a corner and listened to the questions and answers :

" Duval, did you see the accused at six o'clock in the evening ? "

" That is to say, Monsieur le Juge, my wife was at the window. Then she said to me : ' There's Socquardot going by ! ' "

" His presence under your window must have struck her as remarkable since she took the trouble to mention it to you particularly. And did the gait of the accused arouse your suspicion ? "

" I will tell you how it was, Monsieur le Juge. My wife said to me: 'There's Socquardot going by!' Then I looked and said 'Why yes, it's Socquardot!'"

" Precisely! Clerk, write down: At six o'clock in the evening, the couple Duval saw the accused loafing round the house and walking with a suspicious gait."

Monsieur Thomas put a few more questions to the witness, who was a day labourer by occupation: he received replies and dictated to his clerk their translation into judge's jargon. Then the witness listened to the reading of his evidence, signed it, bowed and withdrew.

" Why," I asked, " do you not record the evidence as it is given you instead of translating it into words never used by the witness ? "

Monsieur Thomas gazed at me with astonishment and replied calmly:

" I do not understand your meaning. I record the evidence as faithfully as possible. Every magistrate does. And in all the law reports there is not a single instance of evidence having been altered or distorted by a judge. If, in conformity with the invariable custom of my colleagues, I modify the exact terms used by the witnesses, it is because such witnesses as this Duval, whom you have just heard, express themselves badly, and it would be derogatory to the dignity of justice to record incorrect, low and frequently gross expressions when there is no point in doing so.   But, my dear sir, I think you fail to realize the conditions of a judicial examination. You must bear in mind the object of the magistrate in recording and classifying evidence.   It is not for his own enlightenment alone but for that of the tribunal.   It is not enough for him to see the case clearly, it must be equally clear to the minds of the judges.   He has therefore to bring into prominence those charges which are sometimes concealed beneath the incoherent or diffuse story of a witness or confused by the ambiguous replies of the accused.   If it were to be registered without order or method the most convicting evidence would lose its point and the majority of criminals would escape punishment."

" But surely," I asked, " a proceeding which consists in fixing the wandering thoughts of witnesses must be very dangerous."

"It would be if magistrates were not conscientious. But I never yet met a magistrate who was not deeply conscious of his duty.   And yet I have sat on the Bench with Protestants, Deists and Jews.   But they were magistrates."

" At least you must admit, Monsieur Thomas, that your method possesses one disadvantage : when you read the written account of his evidence to the witness, he can hardly understand it, since you have introduced into it terms he is not accustomed to employ and the sense of which escapes him.   What does your expression ' suspicious gait ' convey to the mind of this labourer ? "

He replied eagerly :

" I have thought of that, and against this danger I have taken the greatest precautions.   I will give you an example.   A short time ago a witness of a somewhat limited intelligence and of whose morals I was ignorant, appeared not to attend to the clerk's reading of the witness's evidence.   I had it read a second time, having urged the deponent to give it his sustained attention.   By what I could see he did nothing of the kind.   Then in order to bring home to him a more correct appreciation of his duty and his responsibility I made use of a stratagem.   I dictated to the clerk one final phrase which contradicted everything that had gone before.   I asked the witness to sign.   Then, just as he was putting pen to paper, I seized his arm.   ' Wretch ! ' I cried, ' you are about to sign a declaration contrary to the one you have made and by so doing to commit a crime '."

" Well ! and what did he say to you ? "

" He replied piteously : ' Monsieur le Juge, you are cleverer than I, you must know best what I ought to write.'

" You see," added Monsieur Thomas, " that a judge anxious to fulfil his function well can guard himself against any danger of making a mistake. Believe me, my dear sir, judicial error is a myth."

A SERVANT'S THEFT

TO HENRI MONOD

A SERVANT'S THEFT

BOUT ten years ago, perhaps more, perhaps less, I visited a prison for women. It was an old chateau built in the reign of Henry IV; and its high slate roofs frowned down upon a dark little southern town on the banks of a river. The governor of the prison had reached the age of superannuation. He wore a black wig and a white beard. He was an extraordinary governor. He had ideas of his own and kindly feelings. He had no illusions concerning the morals of his three hundred prisoners, but he did not consider them to be greatly inferior to the morals of any three hundred women collected haphazard in a town.

" Here as elsewhere we have all sorts and conditions," his gentle, tired glance seemed to say.

As we crossed the courtyard, a long string of prisoners was returning from a silent walk and going back to the workshops. Many of them were old and

of hard, sullen aspect.   My friend Dr. Cabane, who
was with us, pointed out to me that nearly all these
women had characteristic physical defects, that
squinting was not uncommon among them, that
they were degenerates and that nearly all were
marked with the stigma of crime or at least of
misdemeanour.

The governor slowly shook his head.   I saw that
he was disinclined to admit the theories of criminolo-
gists.   He was evidently still convinced that in our
social groups the guilty do not greatly differ from
the innocent.

He took us to the workshops.   We saw the bakers,
the laundresses and the needlewomen at their tasks.
The atmosphere of work and neatness imparted
almost a cheerful air to the place.   The governor
treated the women kindly.   The most stupid and
the most perverse failed to exhaust his patience
and his benevolence.   His opinion was that one
should excuse many things in those with whom one
lives and that one should not ask too much even from
misdemeanants and criminals.   Unlike most persons,
he did not require thieves and procuresses to be
perfect because they were being punished.   He had
little faith in the moral efficacy of punishment, and
he despaired of making his prison a school of virtue.

Being far from the belief that persons are rendered better by suffering, he spared these unfortunate women as much suffering as possible. I do not know whether he was religious, but for him the idea of expiation had no moral significance.

" I give my own interpretation to the rules," he said, " before applying them. I myself explain them to the prisoners. For example, one rule is absolute silence. Now if they were to be absolutely silent they would become mad or imbecile. That such is the object of the rule I cannot think for one moment. I say to them : the rule commands you to keep silent. What does that mean ? It means that the wardresses must not hear you speak. If you are heard you will be punished ; if you are not heard you will incur no reproach. You have not to give me an account of your thoughts. If your words make no more sound than your thoughts then your words are no affair of mine. Thus admonished, they endeavour to speak without, if one may say so, uttering any sound. They are not driven mad and the rule is kept."

I inquired whether his superiors approved of his interpretation of prison rules. He replied that inspectors frequently reproached him, and that then he conducted them to the outer gate and said :

" You see this railing ; it is of wood. If you con-
fined men here, in a week's time there would not be
one left. The idea of escaping never occurs to
women. But it is prudent not to make them furious.
As it is, prison life conduces neither to physical nor
to moral health. I resign my governorship if you
subject them to the torture of silence."

The infirmary and the dormitories, which we
visited next, were in great white-washed halls which
retained nothing of their ancient splendour except
monumental mantelpieces in grey stone and black
marble surmounted by pompous Virtues in high
relief. The figure of Justice the work of some
Italianate Flemish artist of about 1600, with bare
neck and hip protruding through parted drapery,
held suspended from one stout arm its unequally
balanced scales, the plates of which clinked against
each other like cymbals. This goddess seemed to
menace with the point of her sword a little sickly
form lying on an iron bedstead, upon which was a
mattress as thin as a folded towel. It looked like a
child.

" Well ! And are you better ? " asked Dr.
Cabane.

" Oh ! yes, sir, much better."

And she smiled.

" Come then, you must be good and you will get well."

She looked at the doctor with wide eyes full of joy and hope.

" This little girl has been very ill," said Dr. Cabane.

And we passed on.

" What was her offence ? "

" It was no mere offence, it was a crime."

" Ah ! "

" Infanticide."

At the end of a long corridor, we entered an almost cheerful little room, furnished with cupboards and with windows which, devoid of iron bars, looked on to the country.   Here a very pretty young woman was writing at a desk.   Standing near her another with a good figure was looking for a key in a bunch hanging from her waist.   I might have taken them for the governor's daughters.   He informed me that they were two prisoners.

" Did you not notice that they wear prisoner's dress ? "

I had not noticed it, doubtless because they did not wear it like the others.

" Their dresses are better made and they wear smaller caps which show their hair."

P

"It is very difficult," replied the old governor, "to prevent a woman showing her hair when it is beautiful. These two are subject to the ordinary regulations and compelled to work."

"What are they doing?"

"One is keeper of the records and the other is librarian."

There was no need to ask: their offences were crimes of passion. The governor made no secret that he preferred criminals to misdemeanants.

"I know some criminals," he said, "who are as it were aloof from their crime. It was a flash in their life. They are capable of straightforwardness, courage and generosity. I could not say as much for my thieves. Their mediocre and commonplace wrongdoing is woven into the very tissue of their existence. They are incorrigible. And the baseness which was the cause of their misdemeanour reveals itself over and over again in their conduct. The penalty imposed on them is relatively light, and, as they have little sensibility either physical or moral, they generally bear it easily."

"But it does not follow," he added quickly, "that these unhappy creatures are unworthy of pity and do not deserve to have an interest taken in them. The longer I live the more clearly do I see that

the so-called criminal is in reality merely unfortunate."

He took us into his room and told a warder to
bring him prisoner 503.

"I am going to show you something," he said,
"which I entreat you to believe has not been
arranged purposely for you; it will inspire you
doubtless with some novel reflections on lawbreak-
ing and its punishment. What you are about to
see and hear I have seen and heard a hundred
times in my life."

A prisoner accompanied by a wardress entered
the room. She was a young peasant girl, rather
pretty, sweet and simple looking.

"I have some good news for you," said the
governor. "The President of the Republic, having
been told of your good conduct, remits the re-
mainder of your sentence. You will be liberated
on Saturday."

She was listening with her mouth half open, her
hands clasped below the waist. But she was not
quick to grasp ideas.

"Next Saturday you will leave this place. You
will be free."

This time she understood, her hands rose in a
gesture of distress, her lips trembled.

" Is it true that I must go away ?   Then what will become of me ?   Here I was fed, clothed and everything.   Could you not tell the good gentleman that it is better for me to stay where I am ? "

Gently but firmly the governor showed her that she could not refuse the mercy shown her ; then he informed her that on her departure she would receive a certain sum, ten or twelve francs.

She went out weeping.

I inquired what she had done.

He turned over a register.

" 503.   She was servant in a farmhouse. . . . She stole a petticoat from her mistress. . . . A theft committed by a servant. . . . On such offences, you must know, the law is very severe."

EDMÉE, OR CHARITY WELL
BESTOWED

TO H. HARDUIN

EDMÉE, OR CHARITY WELL
BESTOWED

ORTEUR, the founder of *l'Etoile*, the political and literary editor of *La Revue Nationale* and of *Le Nouveau Siècle Illustré*, Horteur, having received me in his editorial room, from the depths of his editorial arm-chair addressed me thus:

" My good Marteau, write me a story for the special number of *Le Nouveau Siècle*. Three hundred lines for New Year's Day. Something amusing with a high society atmosphere."

I told Horteur that that was not in my line, at least not in the sense in which he understood it, but that I was prepared to write him a story.

" I should like it to be entitled," he said, " a tale for the rich."

" I should prefer a tale for the poor."

" That is what I mean. A tale to inspire the rich with pity for the poor."

" But that is precisely what I object to. I do not want the rich to have pity on the poor."

" Curious ! "

" No, it is not curious, but scientific. In my opinion the pity of the rich for the poor is an insult and a denial of human brotherhood. If you wish me to address the rich I shall say : ' Spare the poor your pity : they have no use for it. Wherefore pity and not justice ? You have an account with them. Settle it. This is no question of sentiment. It is a matter of economics. If that which you are pleased to give them is calculated to prolong their poverty and your wealth, the gift is iniquitous and the tears you mingle with it will not render it just. "You must make restitution," as the attorney said to the judge after good Brother Maillard's sermon. You give alms in order to avoid making restitution. You give a little in order to keep much, and you gloat over it. For a like reason the tyrant of Samos threw his ring into the sea. But the Nemesis of the gods declined to receive the offering. A fisherman brought back the tyrant his ring in a fish's belly. And Polycrates was despoiled of all his wealth '."

" You are joking."

" I am not joking. I want to make the rich understand that they are benevolent on the cheap, that their generosity costs them little, that they only make the creditor curl his lip, and that such is not the way to conduct business. It is an opinion which may be of use to them."

" And these are the ideas you propose to express in *Le Nouveau Siècle* in order to increase the circulation! Not a bit of it my friend! Not a bit of it!"

" Why do you insist on the rich man assuming towards the poor an attitude different from that which he assumes towards the rich and powerful ? He pays the rich what he owes them, and if he owe them nothing he pays them nothing. That is honest. If he be honest let him do the same for the poor. And do not say that the rich owe the poor nothing. I do not believe that a single rich man thinks so. It is upon the extent of the debt that opinions begin to differ. And no one is in a hurry to solve the problem. It is thought better to leave the matter vague. Every one is aware that he is in debt. But what he owes is uncertain, and so from time to time a little is paid on account. That is called philanthropy, and it is profitable."

" But, my dear fellow, there is no common sense in what you have been saying. Possibly I am more of a Socialist than you, but I am practical. To relieve suffering, to prolong a life, to redress some particle of social injustice is to attain a result. The little good one does is at any rate done. It is not everything but it is something. If the story I ask you to write goes home to the hearts of a hundred of my rich subscribers and induces them to give it will be so much won from evil and suffering. Thus little by little the lot of the poor is rendered bearable."

" Is it good for the lot of the poor to be bearable ? Poverty is indispensable to wealth and wealth to poverty. These two evils beget one another and foster one another. The condition of the poor does not need to be improved, but to be suppressed. I will not encourage the rich to give alms, because their alms are poisoned, because their alms do good to the giver and harm to the receiver, because in short, wealth being of itself hard and cruel it must not put on the deceitful appearance of kindness. Since you wish me to write a story for the rich, I will say to them : ' Your poor are your dogs whom you feed in order that they may bite. Your bedesmen become the hounds of the propertied classes who bay at the proletariat. The rich give only to those who ask. The workers ask nothing, and they receive nothing '."

" But the infirm, the aged and the orphaned ? . . ."

" They have the right to live. For them I would not excite pity, I would appeal to justice."

" All this is mere theorizing! To return to reality. You will write me a New Year's Story, and you may introduce a suggestion of Socialism. Socialism is quite fashionable. It is even a distinction. Of course I am not referring to the Socialism of Guesde or of Jaurès, but to a moderate Socialism such as men of the world intelligently and rightly oppose to collectivism. Have some young faces in your story. It will be illustrated and readers like pictures to be pleasing. Bring a young girl on the scene, a charming young girl. It will not be difficult."

" No, it is not difficult."

" Could you not introduce a little chimney-sweep ? I have an illustration ready, a coloured engraving, which represents a young girl giving alms to a little chimney-sweep on the steps of the Madeleine. This would be an opportunity for using it. . . . It is cold, the snow is falling : the pretty girl is dropping a coin into the chimney-sweep's hand. Can you see it ? "

" I see it."

" You will develop that theme."

" I will develop it. The little sweep, in a transport of gratitude throws his arms round the girl's neck. She happens to be the daughter of the Comte de Linotte. He gives her a kiss, imprinting on the charming child's cheek a little round O of soot. A perfectly enchanting little O, quite round and quite black. He loves her. Edmée (her name is Edmée) is not indifferent to so sincere and ingenuous an attachment. . . . I fancy the idea is sufficiently pathetic."

" Yes. You will be able to make something of it."

" You encourage me to continue. On her return to her sumptuous home in the Boulevard Males-herbes, for the first time in her life Edmée is reluctant to wash her face: she would like to preserve the imprint of those lips on her cheek. Meanwhile the little sweep has followed her to her door. Rapt in ecstasy he stands beneath the adorable young girl's window. . . . Will that do ? "

" Why, yes ! "

" I continue. The next morning, lying on her little white bed, Edmée sees the little sweep coming down the chimney. Without any ado he throws himself on the charming child and covers her with little round O's of soot. I omitted to tell you that he is extremely handsome. While thus delightfully occupied he is surprised by the Comtesse de Linotte. She screams, she calls for help. But so absorbed is he that he neither sees nor hears."

" My dear Marteau. . . ."

" So absorbed is he that he neither sees nor hears. The Comte hastens into the room. He has the soul of a true aristocrat. He takes up the little sweep by the seat of his breeches . . . and throws him out of the window——"

" My dear Marteau. . . ."

" I hasten to conclude. . . . Nine months later the little sweep married the high-born maiden. And it was high time too. Such was the result of charity well bestowed."

" My dear Marteau, you have amused yourself long enough at my expense."

" Not a bit of it. I must finish. Having married Mademoiselle de Linotte, the little sweep became a papal count and was ruined on the Turf. To-day he is a stove dealer at Montparnasse in the Rue de la Gaîté. His wife keeps his shop and sells stoves at eighteen francs apiece payable in eight months."

" My dear Marteau it isn't the least bit funny."

" Beware, my dear Horteur. What I have just told you is really Lamartine's *Chute d'un Ange* and Alfred de Vigny's *Eloa*. And, taking it all round, it is better than your tearful tales, which make folk believe that they are very kind when they are not kind at all, that they do good when they do nothing of the sort, that it is easy for them to be benevolent when it is the most difficult thing in the world. My story is moral. Moreover it is optimistic and ends well. For, in her shop in the Rue de la Gaîté, Edmée found the happiness which in amusements and festivities she would have sought in vain, had she been married to a diplomat or an officer. . . . My dear editor, are we agreed: Will you have *Edmée, or Charity well Bestowed* for the *Nouveau Siècle Illustré?* "

" You ask me that in all seriousness ? . . . "

" In all seriousness I ask you. If you will not have my story, I will publish it elsewhere."

" Where ? "

" In some high class journal."

" I dare you to do so."

" You will see."

The *Figaro,* under the editorship of Monsieur de Rodays, published *Edmée ou La Charité bien placée.* It was, so to speak, offered as a New Year's gift to the readers of that paper.

www.ingramcontent.com/pod-product-compliance
Lightning Source LLC
Chambersburg PA
CBHW050509260626
47157CB00004B/1257